D1711517

STATE vs. LASSITER

Paul Levine

DISCARD

Published by Nittany Valley Productions, Inc.
COPYRIGHT © 2013 Paul J. Levine
All rights reserved
Cover design by www.damonza.com
Interior design by Steven W. Booth, www.GeniusBookServices.com

This book is a work of fiction. Names, characters, places and incidents are either products of the author's imagination or used fictitiously. Any resemblance to actual events, locales or persons, living or dead, is entirely coincidental. All rights reserved. No part of this publication can be reproduced or transmitted in any form or by any means, electronic or mechanical, without permission in writing from Paul J. Levine. www.paul-levine.com

BOOKS BY PAUL LEVINE

THE JAKE LASSITER SERIES

To Speak for the Dead
Night Vision
False Dawn
Mortal Sin
Riptide
Fool Me Twice
Flesh & Bones
Lassiter
Last Chance Lassiter
State vs. Lassiter

THE SOLOMON & LORD SERIES

Solomon vs. Lord
The Deep Blue Alibi
Kill All the Lawyers
Habeas Porpoise

STAND-ALONE THRILLERS

Impact
Ballistic
Illegal
Paydirt

For Marcia…love blooms ever brighter.

"*There are four kinds of homicide: felonious, excusable, justifiable, and praiseworthy.*"
—Ambrose Bierce

"*Have you a criminal lawyer in this burg?*"
"*We think so but we haven't been able to prove it on him yet.*"
—Carl Sandburg

In Memoriam

As this book went to press in August 2013, Elmore Leonard, a giant of crime fiction, died at age 87. Leonard influenced several generations of writers…this one included. I always tried to follow his rules, especially "Leave out the part that readers tend to skip." And this one: "If it sounds like writing, I rewrite it." Leonard was the first recipient of the John D. MacDonald Fiction Award. I was the second. A distant second. Rest in peace, Dutch.

Paul Levine
Miami
September 1, 2013

1

Beach Bum

I woke up spitting sand. Someone was kicking me in the ribs.

"You alive, pal?"

I lifted my head and shielded my eyes against the molten fireball rising from the ocean. Squinting into the sun, I saw a tanned young guy standing over me. Khaki shorts, white shirt with epaulets and a badge. His utility belt held a crackling radio. Beach Patrol. Glorified lifeguards with Tasers.

The guy dug a sneaker into my gut. "C'mon, get up."

"Knock it off or I'll break your leg." I licked my parched lips and tasted blood.

What the hell happened last night?

I'd been with Pamela. My lover and, conveniently enough, my banker at Great Southern. It should have been a night of drinks, dinner, and sex. We'd done the drinking, but then came the accusations and denials. A shadowy memory crept up, like fog over the shoreline.

"What are you hiding, Pam?"

"Screw you, Jake! You're not gonna pin this on me."

"You're the one moving the money."

"Bastard!"

I remembered her raking me across the cheek with a handful of manicured nails. Now, touching my face, I felt tracks of dried blood. Then what happened? How'd I get here, face down on the beach? Hadn't I rented a suite at the Fontainebleau? Until the blow-up, weren't Pam and I celebrating the best fiscal report in the history of the Law Offices of Jacob Lassiter. Esq.? Weren't we in love? At least, I thought we were.

"Unless you fell out of a boat, you're breaking the law." Mr. Beach Patrol again. "City Code section three-seventy-two, subsection B-1. No overnight camping on the beach."

I let my head fall back to the sand. "Camping? Does it look like I'm toasting marshmallows?"

Sea birds pecked at the wet sand near my head. Breakfast time. I felt chilled. The incoming tide splashed my bare left foot. There was a brown suede shoe on my right foot. No sign of the left shoe. I wore taupe dress slacks and an unbuttoned blue silk shirt. My belt was missing. Had I been stripping for a nighttime swim when I passed out?

"On your feet, pal. Last time I'm gonna tell you." He nudged me again with a sneaker.

"Go pound sand." I laughed at my little joke and hacked up what tasted like the syrupy remnants of several margaritas.

"I'm responsible for Tenth Street Beach, and I'm giving you a direct order."

Tenth Street?

Meaning I'd walked 30 blocks from the Fontainebleau before taking a snooze at the high tide line.

"Lemme alone," I said.

"You want to get run-over? A half-track will be clearing seaweed in about five minutes."

He drew his foot back to kick me again. I grabbed his other ankle and jerked hard. He tumbled backward, arms wheeling, fell to the ground.

I got to one knee, but my head was filled with bowling balls, and I never made it to my feet. Flat on his back, Mr. Beach Patrol snaked the Taser from its holster and nailed me. I spasmed and toppled sideways, a buffalo hit by lightning. The pain rattled my teeth, and my brain blazed with a light brighter than the rising sun.

∾

Ten minutes later, I was handcuffed and sitting cross-legged on the beach when a cop tricycle – okay, a three-wheel all-terrain vehicle pulled up –

spraying me with sand. The Beach Patrol biker, an older guy with sergeant stripes, whispered to the young guy who'd microwaved me.

I couldn't make out much. The words "Lassiter" and "cops" and "Fontainebleau" were being tossed around.

"You guys want to give me a ticket and get this over with?" I said.

They kept whispering.

"How 'bout cutting me a break and go piss on some tourists with jellyfish stings?"

The young guy let out a long, low whistle, then glanced at me. The sergeant clapped him on the back and said, "Well done," as if he'd just busted John Dillinger or maybe cleaned all the bird poop from the beach.

"Mr. Lassiter, this is more serious than a ticket," the sergeant said.

"C'mon, I was just sleeping off some tequila."

"Somebody back at the Fontainebleau wants to talk to you."

"Who?"

"Detective Barrios, you know him?"

"Yeah. Why's he want to see me?"

The sergeant and his pals exchanged *get-a-load-of-this-guy* looks. "Why do you think, Mr. Lassiter?"

"Not a clue."

George Barrios was chief of Miami Beach Homicide.

What the hell could he want with me?

2

The Sorrento Penthouse

Two Miami Beach cops escorted me into the penthouse suite. Pamela Baylins lay on the floor, her eyes open and protruding, her legs splayed from beneath her black sequined mini, the same dress she wore to dinner last night. A tall, strong woman in life, she suddenly looked small and frail. A discarded and broken doll.

I felt the rush of my heart, blood pounding through my veins. I felt as if I were falling down a mine shaft, narrow and deep. My knees buckled, and a uniformed cop propped me up by grabbing the handcuffs behind my back. I gasped, tried to say something – I'm not sure what – but my throat was filled with cotton. I tore against the handcuffs. Again, I don't know why, the movement was involuntary. Like a rodeo bull cinched with a leather strap, I felt as if my torso was constricted, taking my breath away. Shock mixed with sorrow and my vision blurred with tears.

I'd been at murder scenes and I'd watched autopsies performed. But none involved someone I loved. Now, I was as motionless as a man stuck in a nightmare.

"You wanna sit down, Mr. Lassiter?" one of the cops said.

"Let him stand," said another.

I scanned the cops' hard, cold faces, then looked back at Pamela. Pink spots dotted her cheeks and her eyelids. Her tongue jutted out the side of her mouth, and bloody mucus dangled from both nostrils. A man's black leather belt was cinched around her neck.

Instinctively, I lifted my cuffed hands and felt for my own belt, even though I already knew the answer. The cops watched as I found nothing but empty loops.

I'd defended enough murder trials to know where this was going. I tried to put off all notions of grief and loss in order to concentrate. I needed to clear my mind and take it all in. If I didn't, I could do a lifetime of mourning in a prison cell.

We were in the living room of the suite. There were no overturned chairs or broken glassware. The welcome basket of fruit and wine was still wrapped in plastic on a cocktail table. Floor-to-ceiling windows overlooked the Atlantic. Blue skies and sun-dappled turquoise waters outside. Blood and ugliness inside.

Pamela's long, frosted hair was tangled beneath her head. Hair that she used to toss with a feminine shake of the head. First the big laugh, then the shake, her hair flying as if riding in a convertible down Collins Avenue on a Spring day.

In life, Pamela's features were in constant motion. Woman of a thousand smiles. Eyes that brightened when she spoke. A rare bird who could talk business or baseball or sex and could play at all three.

I was vaguely aware of movement around me. The quiet, hushed efficiency of a crime scene. Techs combed the carpet. A photographer clicked off dozens of shots. A young Hispanic man in a polo shirt with the logo of the Medical Examiner's office peered into Pamela's eyes. Looking for a cloudy film. A preliminary method of establishing time of death. Jamming a thermometer into her liver for a more precise determination would wait until the body was back at the morgue.

Uniformed cops roamed the two-story suite, whistling at the extravagance of the place. We were on the main level. Three thousand square feet, wide open from the fully equipped kitchen – as if anyone came here to cook – to the oceanfront windows.

"Got a swimming pool on the patio," one cop was saying.

"You mean a Jacuzzi," another said.

"Yeah, that, too. But a real pool."

A crime scene tech trotted down the stairs from the bedroom level. Pamela and I had planned to spend the night in the master bedroom upstairs. Drinking champagne and making love and getting silly over the whole damn luxuriousness of the place. Now, she was dead, and cops were watching me with cynical eyes, judging the sincerity of my grief and confusion.

Did I go pale? Did my face register shock or horror or grief?

Or guilt?

I couldn't tell. I just stood there. Numb and dumb. Gaping. Aching. Stunned into an empty silence. A creeping sense of self-loathing and regret. If we hadn't argued, if I hadn't left the suite, this never could have happened.

A plainclothes detective whispered something to the photographer who then aimed the camera at my face and snapped off half a dozen pictures. He asked me to turn so he could catch my profile. A better angle for the scratches on my cheek.

I did as I was told.

A female tech in cargo pants and a CMB cop t-shirt knelt in front of me and turned my cuffs inside out, collecting sand in a plastic bag. Another tech in surgical gloves, armed with cotton swabs, said, "Would you please open wide, sir?" She swiped the inside of my gums.

The man in the M.E. polo shirt was scraping residue from under Pamela's fingernails. I caught sight of myself in a wall mirror, saw the dried blood on my face where she had scraped me, knew just how the test would turn out. My DNA would be found under Pamela's nails.

"Want to talk about it, Jake?"

I turned and saw George Barrios. He was close to 60, with a shiny bald head and burly forearms tanned the color of polished chestnuts. He'd been with the Sheriff's Department back in the cocaine cowboy days of the 1980's. *Marielitos* with machine guns. Colombians chopping up enemies with machetes. Bodies stacked in a Burger King truck when the old morgue ran out of space.

Barrios was closing out his career as chief homicide detective of Miami Beach. When there's a killing at the Fontainebleau – the victim a prominent young downtown banker like Pamela – well, you call in Barrios. I'd cross-examined him a number of times over the years and never caught him in a lie. He was tenacious and patient and thorough. His eyes had a concerned look, as if he'd like to help me. Oh, Barrios was damn good at cop work.

"I didn't do it, George."

"Didn't ask if you did. The suite is registered to you. Just wanted you to I.D. her, give us any leads to find the killer."

Right, I thought. And Javert just wanted to find who stole the loaf of bread.

"Pamela Baylins," I said. "But you already know that."

"Want to tell me what happened?"

My head throbbed. Pamela was dead.

Pamela.

Two nights ago, we'd romped the night away in her condo, then talked about a Fall cruise through the Greek islands. It had been her idea, and I'd said yes. We'd already taken a Spring trip I'd planned. A baseball tour along the East Coast, catching games in Baltimore, Washington, Philadelphia, and New York. Pamela didn't like baseball, but went in all the way, buying Orioles and Nationals jerseys, before deciding that the red and white Phillies uniform complemented her complexion. By the time we hit Yankee Stadium, she was spitting sunflower seeds like a veteran catcher in the bullpen.

Then last night…

The weekend was to be a romantic getaway without even leaving town. A client I'd once walked on a marijuana possession-with-intent-to-distribute charge worked in P.R. for the Fontainebleau and got us the Sorrento Penthouse gratis. We'd had dinner at Prime 112, the steakhouse favored by NBA teams and hotshot lawyers. In between the first martini and the $30 shrimp cocktail, I'd gotten a call from Barry Samchick, my accountant. He'd been doing my tax returns for 11 years but had never before called on a Saturday night.

"Your trust accounts are screwed up, Jake."

I felt a burning ingot the pit of my gut. It's news every lawyer dreads. Trust accounts hold customers' money…excuse me, clients' money. The Florida Bar will punch your ticket for messing around with dough that doesn't belong to you, even if you've just "borrowed" it for a few days to pay your secretary or your bookie.

"Screwed up how, Barry? You saying money's missing?"

"Just the opposite. One account has too much. Carlos Castillo's. Not a lot, but everything's got to balance to the penny."

I was breathing easier. "Zero it out and transfer the excess to my operating account."

"That's what I thought until I looked at the other accounts."

"Shit. They're out of balance, too?"

"No, but when I downloaded the backup documents from Great Southern Bank, I saw lots of electronic transfers back-and-forth to banks in the Caymans. Do you maintain accounts there?"

"Who do you think I am, Mitt Romney? Of course not."

"The amounts shipped out and sent back were identical. They all balanced, except for the one where too much money came back in."

It had made no sense. I was the only one with the password for electronic transfers. The only other person who even dealt with my trust accounts was my personal banker. *Personal* with a capital "P." As in Pamela. The woman I had been wining dining, and banging. And maybe even adoring. The woman now dead on the floor.

"Would you like a glass of water?" Barrios asked.

I nodded.

"Uncuff him," Barrios ordered a uniformed cop.

When my hands were free, I massaged my wrists and drained the glass of water Barrios handed me. "Am I under arrest?"

"Like my marital life, it's complicated, Jake. Beach Patrol might book you for resisting arrest. But for the homicide, no."

"Not yet," I thought, trying to read his mind.

"So I can leave?"

"Why not help yourself out first and talk about what happened here?"

Screw that. He hadn't answered my question. If the law were a frozen pond, Barrios stood on a thin patch of ice. If I'd been under arrest, he would have read my rights before interrogating me. But he had skated past the question, implying I could leave, but maybe I should just stick around a chat a while to *help myself out.*

I always tell my clients to clam up. There's a poster on my office wall that reproduces a couple lines from Graham Greene's "The Quiet American."

"I never like giving information to the police. It saves them trouble."

Cops are not your friends, I tell my clients. They are trained to trap you, so don't answer their questions, no matter how politely they ask. Anything you say can and *will* be used against you. Here's a wrinkle in the law that's reason enough to keep your mouth shut. Incriminating statements are admissible. But anything helpful you tell the cops is hearsay and won't be repeated in court.

Then there's the problem of the blabbermouth client. Sometimes an innocent client will often stretch the truth or tell innocuous lies to make the story better. In court, the prosecutor will haul out the sledgehammer.

"If the defendant lied about what color Jockeys he was wearing, how can you trust him about anything?"

So, after due consideration, despite knowing all this from more than 20 years dealing with cops and prosecutors, I turned to the veteran homicide detective and said, "Sure, George. What do you want to know?"

3

The Nine Steps of Convicting Yourself

Detective Barrios escorted me onto a balcony the size of a basketball court. The balcony overlooked the Atlantic on one side and the Intercoastal on the other. Sixteen hours earlier, Pamela and I had kissed at the railing, the ocean breeze warm and salty.

Barrios and I hadn't even sat down when the door opened and a woman in a short turquoise tennis dress and matching headband joined us. Emilia Vazquez was Chief of Major Crimes in the State Attorney's office. Probably the best prosecutor between Miami and Orlando. Tall and leggy, she had a sculpted jawline that looked damn good in profile in front of the jury box. I'd tried several cases against her, winning a couple and losing several more. I'd also played tennis against her and had never won a set. A decade ago, I'd also dated her for several months. It ended without shouts or tears; it just ended. Today, I figured she got a call while rushing the net down at Flamingo Park, at

13th and Michigan, ruining her Sunday morning doubles match.

"Emilia, I'm glad to see you," I said.

"Are you?" She tucked a stray strand of hair under the headband and studied me through dark eyes, as hard as obsidian.

"I want you to find whoever did this."

"I'm sure you do."

I didn't like the way she said it. Her tone wasn't sarcastic so much as flat and mechanical.

"She had a guy stalking her. An ex-boyfriend."

"Crowder. We know all about him and we're checking him out."

"Well, that's a start."

"Now, let's see how much you can help us, Jake."

Emilia tried to maneuver me into a seat at a glass breakfast table, so that I would be looking into the morning sun. I stutter-stepped and settled into a chair looking south along the beach with a slice of the Intercoastal on the far side of Collins Avenue. Barrios sat directly across from me, which meant he would start the interrogation. Emilia sat at a 90-degree angle to my right so that my eyes would have to swing back and forth, never being able to see them both simultaneously.

That unnerves some people. Not me. As a trial lawyer, I'm an actor on a stage in-the-round, so I'm not bothered by folks staring into my ears or at my butt, should they be so inclined. But this was different. These weren't spectators judging my performance. These were suspicious bloodhounds.

"You and the decedent checked in yesterday at 4:25 p.m.," Barrios began, without consulting his notes. "You got yourself comped on a two thousand dollar a night suite."

"That a crime?" I was staring at the digital recorder Barrios had placed on the table, thinking I ought to go light on the sarcasm. What I really should do was shut up. No one has ever talked a cop into believing he is innocent.

"You asked the concierge to book an 8 o'clock reservation at Prime 112. Then you called room service and ordered a bottle of Cristal and stone crab appetizers for two. The waiter set up the order on the balcony off the second floor master bedroom. The decedent drank the champagne. You had two beers from the refrigerator."

"You sure it wasn't the other way around?"

"Only if those lipstick stains on the champagne glass were yours."

While the techs had been swabbing and dusting and clicking photos, Detective Barrios had been doing his homework, and I had been sweating.

"You used the Jacuzzi," he continued. "Had sex. Showered, dressed and caught a cab in front of the hotel at 7:42 p.m. The decedent was wearing the same outfit as when she was killed."

I was supposed to be impressed, but it wasn't working. There were security cameras at the valet parking kiosk that would have picked us up getting into the cab. The tapes would show the time and what Pamela was wearing.

As for the Jacuzzi, those were just assumptions, probably from the wet towels. Except it had just been me. Pamela declined, saying she didn't want to ruin her hair. But there'd been no sex, despite my hopes for romps both before and after dinner. As it turned out, we didn't have time before going to Prime 112. After dinner, there was plenty of time, but we'd been squabbling instead of canoodling. So, Lieutenant Columbo just screwed the pooch on that one. Had he just been guessing?

"This sex we had," I said to the detective. "Was it good for me?"

He looked at me with tired eyes. "That's pretty flippant for someone whose girlfriend was just murdered."

"Lover. Pam was my lover. I'm too old for girlfriends."

Emilia leaned forward and exhaled a little puff of air. I'd almost forgotten she was there. "You don't seem overly upset by her death." She sounded personally offended.

"You have no idea how I feel, Emilia. But I know where you two are coming from."

"Do tell."

"Step one of the nine steps of interrogation. *Positive Confrontation*. You're showing me you already have all this stuff, and I'm supposed to wonder what else you have."

"What do you think we have?" Barrios said, resuming control. He probably preferred the prosecutor to keep quiet. Her turn would come in court.

"Credit card records from the restaurant," I said. "You'll know what we ate and drank and how big a tip I left. You probably already woke up the maître d' who told you that we argued at the table."

"As did your server and the couple next to you who ordered Kobe beefsteak for two."

Showing off again, I thought.

"You continued arguing in the cab on the way back to the hotel and right through the front door into the lobby."

And all this time I thought doormen were supposed to be discreet.

"The security camera at the front door picked up your body language, and it doesn't take a lip reader to de-code what the decedent said to you."

"Millions of couples argue every day, but damn few kill each other."

"'Fuck you, Jake.' That's what she said as you came into the hotel."

"If I killed every woman who told me the same thing, I'd be in the books with Jack the Ripper."

"Do you frequently compare yourself to a serial killer who preyed on women?" Emilia broke in.

"I was making a joke."

"As usual, an inappropriate one."

"Is this gonna get personal? Between you and me, I mean?"

Emilia gritted her teeth. Or maybe her jaw muscles just danced like that whenever she was in her tough prosecutor mold. "Your girlfriend. Excuse me, your lover has just been murdered, and you're cracking jokes."

"It's a defense mechanism, okay? It's the way I deal with loss."

"C'mon, Jake. I know you. You have a hard bark, and if you have any heart, it's packed in concrete."

"Absolutely untrue. And pretty damn offensive, too."

In truth, I was forcing myself not to think about Pam. Trying to postpone the pain in order to concentrate. If I allowed myself to think about her, feel the heat of her breath, hear the chimes of her laugh, I could not fend off the cross-examining detective. An even deeper truth was that I cared for her. Deeply and more all the time. The relationship was going somewhere. I respected Pam's intelligence and accomplishments. What made our argument last night so painful was the feeling of betrayal. I had trusted her with my clients' money. What had she done? Then there was my own guilt for the failure to protect her. A wave of conflicting emotions.

"Jake, tell us what you and Ms. Baylins argued about," Barrios said. Double-teaming me.

"Why don't you ask the cab driver? Or the maître 'de. Or that couple eating the Kobe steak."

"We know it had to do with your bank accounts. You accused Ms. Baylins of mishandling your accounts. She accused you of stealing from clients. Is that about it?"

"I've never stolen from a client."

"So you must have been indignant at the allegation?"

"Was I?"

"I'd be furious."

I smiled at that. We'd just moved to step two. *Theme Development.* It's where the cop looks through the eyes of the suspect and tries to establish a common bond. The cop empathizes and gains the suspect's trust. Maybe he even says something stripping away all blame from the suspect: *"Hell, who could blame a man for killing a woman who did that?"*

"I don't steal from my clients. And I don't kill my lovers, okay George?"

"But you have a temper, Jake. You can't deny that."

Wow. That was fast. Step three. *Stopping Denials.* In cop school, they teach them to interrupt all denials. They don't want the suspect to become wedded to his story, because that will make it harder to get to step nine of the solid gold inter-rogation: *The Confession*.

"I don't have a temper," I said.

Emilia barked out a little laugh. "I remember bar fights. Jeez, one was poolside of the Hyatt at the Bar convention."

"That's three times, Emilia."

"What is?"

"Your personal attacks. First, I have an inap-propriate sense of humor. Next, no heart so I can't feel pain. Now, you're practically testifying about my alleged violence."

"Facts are facts."

"C'mon, let's get it out on the table!" I snapped.

She fiddled with a turquoise wristband. Terry cloth to catch the sweat in a heated tennis match. But just now, I was the one sweating. "Get what out, Jake?"

"Ah jeez. You and me. Our past."

"Go on." Gesturing toward the tape recorder. "Say what you have to say."

"We were…how shall I put this? Involved?"

She shook her head. "Overstates the case."

"Dating, then."

"Such a quaint term, Jake. Images of ice cream sundaes and Saturday afternoon movies."

Barrios leaned back in his chair. No way he wanted a piece of this.

"Okay, we weren't involved," I said. "We weren't even dating. We were…?"

"Fucking, Jake. We fucked off and on."

Call me old-fashioned, but I recoil when a smart, olive-skinned beauty with a dozen years of parochial school and a law degree from Georgetown–a place crawling with Jesuits–drops the F-bomb.

"Whatever you call it, Emilia, you can't be objective about me."

"It was ten years ago, Jake. The statute of limitations has expired."

Next she'd be saying she didn't remember it. But I did. And she was downplaying the relationship. There were some blissful days and steamy nights. So why didn't it amount to more? Emilia was so damn competitive. And truth be told, so was I. She didn't try to mold herself to my needs, nor I to hers. Compromise was not in either of our vocabularies. We each liked to win, not to tie.

Pamela Baylins was the opposite. She folded herself into my life, easy and acquiescent. Restaurants, movies, trips. *"Whatever you want to do, Jake."*

With Pamela, you got what she figured you wanted her to be. Which meant, now that her apparent thievery came to light, I really didn't know her at all. She was so unlike Emilia, who was combative and challenging, the living embodiment of a Helen Reddy song.

"I am Woman, hear me roar."

Like any good trial lawyer, Emilia loved to argue. But unlike some, she couldn't leave it in the courthouse.

"Our brief time together is legally irrelevant," Emilia said now. "Hell, it was irrelevant at the time."

"Not to me," I said, honestly. "And that means you shouldn't be interrogating me."

"Who's interrogating? You're giving a voluntary statement and you're free to go at any time. Do you want to go, Jake? Do you want a lawyer? A beer? Anything?"

"Face it. You have a conflict of interest, Emilia."

"Why? I thought you were just a witness. Are you saying you're a suspect?"

"You and your damn lawyer games. This is why we didn't get along."

"We got along fine, Jake as long as all we did was fuck after Happy Hour."

That word again, coming from those full, seductive lips. The Trevi Fountain, spouting piss.

"I didn't realize it until now, but you're steamed because I stopped seeing you."

"So I want to frame you for murder?"

"Who knows?"

"For the record, you didn't stop seeing me. I dropped you when I met that English professor from Boca."

"The cross dresser?"

She slammed her hand down on the table and the recorder toppled over. "He was playing 'Tootsie' in Regional Theater."

I turned to Detective Barrios. "Is this what you two cooked up? Good cop, insane cop?"

He gave me a little smile as if he'd just solved a Brinks' hijacking. "You ask me, you two are made for each other."

"Oh, please, detective." Emilia shot Barrios a look that could leave bruises.

"I mean it. The scent of arousal is in the air."

"I'm not gonna answer any more questions with her here," I said.

Emilia stood and threw her hands up in surrender. "In order to make Mr. Lassiter comfortable, I'll leave."

Good. I'd rather face one inquisitor than two.

She nodded to Barrios and started for the balcony door. Little turquoise balls were fastened to the top of her tennis socks and bounced over the back of her sneakers.

When she reached the door, she turned to me. "I can re-assign the case to Abe Socolow, Jake."

"Great. I've kicked his ass in court so many times, he brings a pillow to court."

"Or how about Abby Press? She's new to major crimes, but she's fair and honest."

"You know damn well I dated Abby for a year."

"Ended badly, didn't it? Problem is, Jake, you've left a trail of damage wherever you go."

"Pick whoever you want, Emilia. The best you've got, because I didn't do this."

"Did you love her?"

"Who, Abby?"

"Pamela, you idiot!"

"Is that a personal or professional question?"

"Screw you, Jake!"

"I cared for her. She was my lady. We had potential together. I didn't kill her, and I damn well want you to nail the bastard who did."

"I promise to do exactly that, Jake," Emilia said. "Nail the bastard. Even if it's you."

4

Hell No!

When the balcony door closed behind Emilia Vazquez, George Barrios gave me a half-smile and a little shrug.

Ah, women, he seemed to be saying.

Now, it was just the two of us guys. But the savvy detective simply picked up where my ex-whatever-she-was left off.

"Emilia's right about that temper of yours," he said, evenly.

"No way, George."

"C'mon, Jake. You have a propensity for violence."

"A propensity, is it?"

"I remember when you got arrested for slugging a cop."

"A case of mistaken identity," I said.

"Bullshit. That was you."

"Yeah, but when I hit him, I didn't know he was a cop."

"As a lawyer, your reputation is pretty rough."

"Thank you."

"You're a killer in the courtroom."

"Hey George, they don't call us sharks for our ability to swim."

Barrios made a notation in his little notebook. Maybe I'd said something inculpatory. Or maybe he was reminding himself to buy a gallon of milk on the way home.

"Last night, you got back to the hotel just after 10 p.m. Did you go straight to your suite?"

"Pam wasn't in the mood for the Boom Boom Room."

"Boom Boom's been closed for decades, Jake."

"Why wasn't I informed? I was hoping to see Sinatra."

"Later, you left the suite."

"Obviously. The kid who thinks he's Michael Phelps found me on the beach."

"What time did you leave the hotel?"

"Don't know."

That was true. I'd had too much to drink and had argued too long with Pam. But even if I knew the time, my answer would have been the same. I was in dangerous territory, treading carefully. If the M.E. established time of death earlier than my departure from the suite, I'd be screwed. And I had as much faith in those T.O.D. calculations as I do in a two-week weather forecast.

"C'mon, Jake," Barrios prompted me. "You must have some idea. How long were you back in the room before you left?"

He really wanted to pin me down, and I wanted to squirm away. "No idea, George."

"Why'd you leave in the middle of the night?"

"I didn't say it was the middle of the night."

"Okay. Whenever you left, why? Were you still arguing?"

I could deny it, but the scratches on my face would reveal that lie. For all I know, guests in the adjoining suite might have heard us, too.

"We had words," I admitted.

"Care to share some of those words?"

"Same stuff you've already heard. The trust accounts."

"But why'd you leave?" Barrios hammered again.

"I'd been drinking. A lot. We both had. Best I recall, I wanted to walk on the beach, clear my head."

"Were you afraid of what you might do to Pam?"

"As I recall, Pam suggested I take off for a while, get some air."

"So was she afraid what you'd do if you stayed in the suite?"

"Aw, jeez, George. You gotta know better than that."

"What about your belt? Why'd you leave that in the room?"

"I don't remember taking it off. Maybe I was getting ready for bed, then decided to leave for a while."

"Did you strike Pam with the belt?"

"Of course not."

"Wrap it around her throat?"

"Way too early for that question. You haven't even softened me up yet."

"Maybe you didn't intend to kill her. Scare her a bit is all. Convince her to keep her mouth shut about your bank accounts."

"Where'd you learn your interrogation skills, George? *Law & Order?*"

"How'd you get those marks on your face?" he fired right back.

"Pam slapped me."

"Slapped?"

"A combo slap and scratch. The way a cat swipes with its paws."

"Had you hit her first?"

"My Granny taught me a long time ago that only a low-life scumsucker hits a woman."

"So that's a no?"

"A hell no!"

The book tells them to try and overcome my denials, after which the cop would become my pal and help me out. Then I would be expected to lose my resolve, which I'd show by dropping my head into my hands, maybe even crying. Barrios would pat me on the back and offer alternative motives, one of which would be understandable and maybe even socially acceptable, the other one morally repugnant. I would be expected to choose the acceptable motive – he wouldn't care as long as I admitted the killing – and he could sharpen his pencil for a signed confession. I sure as hell wasn't going that route.

"Did you push or shove her?" Barrios demanded.

"No."

"Grab her hard?"

"I never touched her."

"Then you must have said something to provoke her to scratch you like that."

"I'm sure I did."

"What did you say?"

I dug up the memory. Back in the suite after dinner. Drinking, arguing.

"Dammit, Pam. What games are you playing with the money?"

"It wasn't me!"

"First thing in the morning, we're going over the accounts with Barry Samchick, and you better have some damn good explanations."

"Or what?"

"I'll find the State Attorney on the first tee at Riviera and get your ass fired."

"Try it. And first thing Monday, I'll sue your ass for slander."

I wouldn't repeat that to Barrios. The argument with Pamela gave me two motives for murder. If Pamela was the thief: rage. If I was thief: avoiding detection. Heads, I'm guilty. Tails, I'm screwed and tattooed. I'd already said too much and felt as tense as a man juggling hand grenades.

"I'm gonna exercise my right to remain silent from here on out." I looked toward the Intercoastal, where a shiny white sport fisherman in the 50-foot range was heading toward open water. I wanted to be on board.

Barrios stayed quiet. I hadn't asked for a lawyer, so there was no legal requirement to stop pestering me. We sat, feeling the breeze and the listening to the caw of sea birds.

"Jake, let's try again," Barrios said, after a moment. "Back in the suite, you were arguing and—"

"Forget it, George. I'm done. Either arrest me or let me go home." I stood and he didn't tell me to sit back down. "And in case you don't know it, you were wrong about something. I didn't have sex with Pam yesterday."

For the first time, Barrios looked confused. What the hell had I hit on?

"You're sure?"

"Sex with Pam was pretty damn memorable, so yeah George, I'm sure."

"Are you a jealous man, Jake?"

"No, I don't think so. Why?"

"Maybe I've been wrong about motive."

"What the hell are you talking about?"

"When's the last time you had sex with Ms. Baylins?"

It was suddenly clear. The Medical Examiner had already performed a preliminary physical examination. I said, "You thought we had sex because the M.E. found semen in her vagina, didn't he?"

"He thinks so. It has to be tested in the lab."

"Well, it isn't mine."

"Okay, let's assume that's true."

"Isn't it obvious then?" I said, excitedly. "You've got a rapist murderer!"

"Nothing disturbed in the room. No forced entry. No bruising or abrasions or defensive wounds. No evidence of any struggle. No signs of trauma on the victim, other than the strangulation itself. Almost certainly, it was consensual sex."

"Who with!"

"Obviously, I assumed it was you," Barrios said. "But if it wasn't, and if you found out she was having sex with someone else…"

"What?"

"With that temper of yours, well, that could be your motive for murder."

5

My Bentley and Me

Well, didn't I feel like a damn fool? I'd been monogamous with Pamela. I had expected the same in return. There'd been this growing well-spring of care within me for her, and I'd expected that, too, in return. She had indicated it was there. Obviously, I'd been deceived about that as well as about the thievery. The anger spread like a fever across my chest.

We'd been planning more trips together, more time together. The word "love" had been bandied about. I'd even thought about asking her to move in. Now, the damn clinical term "semen in her vagina" was a blade straight to the heart. Did Pamela have sex with someone yesterday before meeting me at the hotel? What kind of woman does that? What kind of man is taken in by that? Wasn't it bad enough being a suspected murderer? Did I have to be a fall guy and a schmuck rolled into one? I fought to contain my rage, like water behind a dam.

I had to get the hell out of there.

I gave a hundred bucks to the Fontainebleau valet – one night's ransom plus tip for my metallic red Bentley Continental convertible – and sailed across the Tuttle Causeway to the mainland. Like a lot in my life the last 18 months, the car was Pam's idea.

"You can't project success driving that old clunker."

"My Eldo's a classic. I'll never give it up."

But now, my beloved 1984 Biarritz Eldorado with its pimpmobile red velvet pillowed uphol-stery sat under a tarp in my driveway. The car had belonged to Strings Hendricks, a Key West piano tuner and marijuana dealer, and I'd taken it as a fee many years ago.

Now, my butt was settled into the black quilted cowhide of the Bentley, just as Pam had intended. She'd found the car at an estate sale the bank was handling.

"It's dirt cheap Jake, $187,500."

"In my world, that buys a lot of dirt."

"But you'll look so good driving it."

At the time, I wondered if Pam meant *she'd* look good riding in it, but I let her talk me into it. I wasn't spending a small fortune on a car, I was marketing myself, she argued. The bank funded the purchase, the loan folding into my law office's line of credit, so I never really noticed the payments. Pam had that way about her, smoothing over the troublesome transactions of life. Lately, I'd felt like an imposter driving the car.

Jake Lassiter, Bentley owner? If my old teammates could see me now, they'd laugh their fat asses off.

Now, top down, buzzing across the Causeway, high above the turquoise waters of Biscayne Bay, I realized I hadn't let myself begin to grieve. When the cops had turned the spotlight on me, I wondered how I appeared to them. Playing back the interrogation in my head, I feared I seemed self-centered and defensive. In reality, I'd been numbed. But I must have looked unmoved by the inert body on the floor.

It had been surreal. Was that really Pamela, the life squeezed out of her? She had been a vibrant, electric presence, bouncing on her toes when she walked, her eyes sparkling when she laughed. A strong, confident woman, she loved wearing sleeveless tops, always showing the smooth slope of her neck and her toned delts. She danced barefoot, drank tequila straight, and slept in the nude. She teared up when Diana Krall sang songs of heartbreak, and she could discuss macroeconomic policies of the International Monetary Fund. In short, she was a total package of a woman, and for a short time, she seemed to enjoy nothing so much as wrapping her long, tanned legs around my hips and squeezing every ounce of pleasure out of me. In return, she offered a myriad of pleasures, and I took them all.

And then what?

Had she become a thief? And a cheating girl-friend, too?

Why?

The Bentley effortlessly climbed the peak of the bridge, and I could see the tiny islands in the bay to the north. It's amazing that some politically-connected developers haven't figured a way to dredge and fill the place, and build high-rise condos on those specks of sand and weeds. Thirty years ago, the artist Christo wrapped the islands in pink polymer sheets. The artsy-fartsy crowd cooed about how the project illuminated the existential link between land and water. I thought it looked like a Halloween prank, someone pouring Pepto Bismol into Biscayne Bay.

Top down, I was cruising at 75 shooting down the slope of the bridge, headed for the mainland. What's the worst that could happen? A speeding ticket would have been the high point of the day.

When I took the southbound exit onto I-95, I called Barry Samchick, my accountant, giving him the shorthand version of the shitstorm that was raining on my head. I told him to get all the trust account records together for a meeting, and he reminded me it was Sunday morning. Had it only been 17 hours since Pamela and I had checked into the Fontainebleau? I told him it couldn't wait, and he said he'd get everything together by noon.

"I don't think you're a thief, Jake."

"Thanks, Barry."

"But murder? That I can see you doing."

"What's that mean?"

"You have a temper."

"The hell I do!"

I hung up on him and tried reaching Doc Charlie Riggs, the retired Medical Examiner. Charlie took a liking to me in my early days in the practice. Or maybe he just felt sorry for me. Usually, he treated defense lawyers with disdain. M.E.'s are government employees with front row seats to the cruelties of mankind. Many are in the prosecutors' pockets. But Doc Riggs was fair and honest and acknowledged that cops and prosecutors and medical examiners made mistakes.

Doc Riggs also helped me find my moral compass, which was rarely pointed due north. Ten years ago, when I confided in him that I was seeing Emilia Vazquez at the same time we had a case against each other, he offered a stern warning not found in the law books: "You can't litigate by day and copulate by night, my boy. At least not with the prosecutor."

Now, I needed Doc Riggs for something more attuned to his expertise: analyzing the forthcoming autopsy report on Pamela Baylins.

Voicemail told me that Doc Riggs was bone-fishing in the Keys and wouldn't turn on his phone until he'd landed a few of the wily critters. As Charlie was a better canoe maker – as we called guys who excavated human torsos – than a fisherman, I didn't expect to hear from him until tomorrow. Feeling alone, I missed and needed the old coot.

I headed through downtown Miami, past quiet skyscrapers where the city's lawyers and bankers plied their mysterious but lucrative trades. Condo towers, too. Some were still lightly occupied from the overbuilding that preceded the Big Dipper of a real estate recession, but savvy investors had bought blocks of the empty apartments and rented them out, awaiting the revival in prices that was now underway.

I had to make another call. It was time to lawyer up. Actually, the time should have been when Detective Barrios started asking questions. But no, good ole Jake Lassiter had to show how smart and tough he was. After all, I'm the guy who, while playing college ball, ran full speed into a goalpost. I shattered my face mask and knocked the post out of kilter so that the crossbar dipped like a power line strung with overfed owls.

By the time I hit South Dixie Highway, I was trying to figure out what lawyer to call. It's the single most important decision for anyone suspected of a crime. I would not be an easy client, and all the bigshot mouthpieces in town would know it. Lawyer defendants are meddlesome, always trying to manage their own cases. An honest self-apprais-al would peg me as worse than most.

I considered waiting for an indictment, then picking a lawyer based on which trial judge caught the case. It's no secret that judges play favorites. Sometimes, it's smart to hire a lawyer who was a Sigma Chi brother of the judge back in their gator-chomping University of Florida days.

But I didn't think I could wait. I needed some-one I could trust now. Someone smart and strong who wouldn't tell me what I wanted to hear. A half dozen names popped into my head. While I was still thinking about it, my cell rang.

Juan Martinez calling. He owned *Havana Banana*, the restaurant situated directly below my second floor "penthouse" office in a broken-down building on South Beach.

"Cops!" Martinez shouted. "Cops broke down your door."

Shit. If they'd have asked, I would have let them in. But Barrios must have gotten a Sunday morning search warrant and sent the storm troop-ers there before I could get to the office.

"Door's split in two," Martinez said.

"What'd they take?"

"How should I know? I was stirring a pot of *ropa vieja*. But Lourdes said she saw them carrying out a computer and boxes of files."

I thanked him, and he told me he'd like my monthly restaurant tab paid first thing in the morning, especially the liquor bill. Apparently, he thought I might be going away for a long while.

Ten minutes later, I was hanging the right hand turn from Douglas Road onto Kumquat in the South Grove. Which is when I heard the insistent *beep-beep-beep* of a car horn behind me. I slowed, checked the rear-view, saw a black Dodge Ram pick-up with a dark tinted windshield easing up on me. What'd this guy want?

The pick-up accelerated and slammed into the rear of my snazzy English convertible. My head whiplashed, and my vision turned into a black night with a starlit sky.

What the hell!

Eyes blurry, I hit the brakes and jammed the Bentley into Park. Unbuckled. Painfully turned and opened the door. My neck felt rigid, frozen in cement. Stepping out, I saw the driver of the Hummer approaching. Big guy with a crew cut. Bigger than me, and I'm an ex-linebacker. He was in his thirties. Jeans, boots, muscle-T, the tattoo of a red and green serpent coiled around his right arm.

He didn't look like he played for the Marlins. So, why the hell was he carrying a baseball bat?

6

Batting Practice

The bat was black with a thin, whippy handle. The guy was white and thick through the chest. My taillight cover was big and red and shaped like a parallelogram, roughly the size of home plate. The guy's first swing shattered it into a hundred pieces of plastic.

His second swing dented the trunk. *Ka-thunk!*

I stood there, gaping. Had I done something to inspire road rage?

"Hey! The hell'd I do to you?"

"You don't know?"

He took three steps toward me, twirling the bat. I backed up, staying just out of range.

"All I know, a maniac is trashing my wheels."

"Rich dipshit faggoty Bentley."

"I love this car," I lied.

"Rich dipshit," he repeated.

"I'm not rich. Not Miami rich, anyway. The car is just for marketing."

He took a short, low swing and smacked the spokes of the right rear wheel, which *pinged* in protest. Two more swings pretzeled them. "Market that, asshole."

"Why you doing this?"

"I loved Pam!"

It took a second. "Crowder? You're Mike Crowder, Pam's ex."

"*Mitch* Crowder, asshole!"

"I'm sorry about Pam. I'm gonna do everything I can to find who killed her."

"Won't have to look far, will you, asshole?" He used an overhead tomahawk swing to crush the trunk.

"You got that wrong, Crowder. I would never have hurt her."

He drew the bat back and approached me. I was two blocks from my house. I could turn and run, but I usually run *into* trouble, not away from it. And there was a chance the guy was faster than me and would split open the back of my skull as I skedaddled.

"Pam tell you about me?" he demanded.

"Told me she got a restraining order."

"Legal bullshit."

"You stalked her. You called her a hundred times a day."

"And you killed her!"

"Who told you that?"

"I own the Iron Asylum, best gym on South Beach. Cops get free memberships. They talk."

"Maybe they ought to haul your ass in for questioning."

"Cops already talked to me, asshole. I got an alibi."

"Want to run it by me?"

"Screw you. She was my soul-fucking-mate!"

"No disrespect, Crowder, but Pam's soulmate probably isn't wiping sweat off Nautilus machines."

"Bastard!"

He came at me, cocking the bat. I fought the urge to move backwards and stepped toward him. His backswing was long and looping and gave me a chance to duck low. The bat whistled over my head, and I dug a short right into his gut. He *whoomphed* but didn't drop the bat. He swung again, backhanded this time, the barrel of the bat clipping the meat of my shoulder. I grimaced and stomped on the instep of his right foot. His head jerked forward, and I hit him with a right uppercut that caught him squarely in the Adam's apple. He gagged and squawked and fell to all fours, dropping the bat.

I twined the fingers of each hand together, making a double fisted hammer and thought about smashing the back of his neck, but I didn't. No killer instinct, no desire to inflict more pain.

"I didn't kill Pam," I said.

He was too busy choking to reply.

I picked up the bat and tossed it into my car. Not so much to keep it away from him, but rather, to have his prints taken from it. Maybe DNA, too. When defending a murder trial, one traditional defense is SODDI. Some Other Dude Did It.

It's a helluva lot better if you can say just who that dude might be.

7

Lard Butt at Home

"Did you kill that girl?" Granny demanded.

"'Course not."

"If you did kill her, I expect you had a good reason."

"I didn't!"

"You can tell me the truth. I'd never turn against you in court."

"Heartwarming to know you'd commit perjury for me."

"What's family for, anywho?"

Ten minutes after I left Mitch Crowder gasping for breath, Granny Lassiter was fixing me breakfast of pecan pancakes, cheese biscuits, ham with red eye gravy rich with black coffee. In my short tenure with the Dolphins, Coach Shula used to call me "lard butt," and there was more truth to it than he knew. Granny couldn't make a pie crust without lard or red eye gravy without ham drippings.

I checked the front window a couple times. No Crowder. No cops. No nosy reporters for the *Mi-*

ami Herald, which probably couldn't afford over-time for a Sunday morning stake-out.

"Ah never liked that girl." Granny's Cracker accent was as thick as the gravy she stirred with a wooden spoon. "A bottle blond with plastic boobs."

"Boobs were real."

"How would you know?"

"Practice, Granny. Practice."

Granny harrumphed her displeasure. "Filthy money!" She tossed a handful of pecans onto the pancakes, which had started bubbling in the pan. "Money, money, money."

"What are you talking about?"

"All the bottle blond knew was money."

"She was a banker, Granny."

"You ask me, she was mixed up in no good."

"Jeez, Granny. What ever happened to not speaking ill of the dead?"

We were in the kitchen of my coral rock bun-galow in Coconut Grove. Granny had moved in a few years ago, leaving her place in Islamorada to help me raise my nephew Kip after my drug-addled half-sister abandoned him. It was an en-core performance for the old gal. After my father was killed in a Key Largo saloon and my mother ran off, Granny raised me, too. Her real name was Dorothea Jane Lassiter. She was most likely my great aunt, but the Lassiter clan wasn't inscribed in the Social Register, so blood lines were often a matter of conjecture and drunken debate.

"She's the one who made you lose your way." Granny tucked several strands of still-black hair under a pink fluorescent band that rode atop her head. She wore green high-top sneakers, canvas shorts and a wife-beater t-shirt from an oyster stand in Key West, with the logo, "Eat 'Em Raw."

I popped into my mouth a warm biscuit, thick with melting cheddar cheese. "Didn't know I was lost."

"I knew it the day you started buying hundred dollar bottles of wine."

"What's that got to do with Pam?"

"Her influence. You were a brew and burger fellow from the time you were fifteen."

"A man grows up."

"That why you went to paté and Cabernet?"

"Don't bust my chops, Granny."

"And those thousand dollar Eye-talian suits you started buying in Bal Harbour."

"My practice picked up. Isn't a man supposed to enjoy the fruits of his labors?"

"Not from Colombian drug dealers."

"Carlos Castillo is a coffee baron."

She harrumphed again and her voice hit its scolding tone. "And you been putting on weight at all them fancy restaurants. I'll bet you'd pass out if you tried humping the causeway."

Meaning running across the Rickenbacker to Key Biscayne. It's a long slog uphill, usually with an ocean breeze in your face, then a slow decline. I used to do it twice a week, though I'd sometimes stop at Jimbo's Shrimp Shack for a beer and smoked fish dip on Virginia Key. These days, I'd never make it that far.

"That woman brought out the lazy in you."

"Jeez, Granny, I been working harder than ever."

"At making money, maybe. Hell, anyone can do that. What have you been doing for your fellow man? How much time you been spending with Kip?"

We'd been having this argument ever since I met Pam. I'd worked my butt off to become a decent trial lawyer. It hadn't been easy. University of Miami Law School, Night Division. I had started my studies after a few undistinguished years with the Dolphins, sitting so far down Shula's bench, my cleats were in Hialeah. Occasionally I played a little linebacker, but more frequently, I just sacrificed my body and sanity on the suicide squads, the kickoff and kick return teams.

I learned the courtroom trade in the Public Defenders' office and continued trying cases in private practice. The problem with criminal defense work is the unassailable fact that nearly every client is guilty. Most cases you plead out and get the best deal possible. Most of the ones you try, you will lose. And some of the cases you win, the client is *factually* guilty, but the state couldn't prove it. It's a disheartening way to make a living.

Then I went into private practice. First, a big firm where I didn't fit in, then I flew solo. Lone gunslingers have an expression about our work: *We only eat what we kill.* So sometimes, you take cases just for the dough. Your case might be infected with legal leprosy and your client might have the personality of a rattlesnake. But you need to pay the rent so you sometimes are stuck petting a reptile or two. In criminal law, if you only accepted cases where your clients were factually innocent, you'd starve. Even worse, your lawyer pals would laugh at you.

୧୨

About 18 months ago, I wandered into a more profitable specialty. Lucked into it, really. My nephew Kip gets the credit for being the rainmaker, the guy who brought in the client. I always taught the kid to do the right thing, even when it's the harder course, and karma will reward you. Not that I necessarily believe it, or that I follow my own advice. It just seems like the right thing to say to a 13-year-old boy who's all hormones and impulses.

Kip was a seventh grader then at Biscayne-Tuttle, the ritzy private school on the bay in Coconut Grove. A wiry ball of motion who didn't fit in easily with any of the cliques. Not a star athlete or an honor student. Not a rap artist in the school's talent show, and though he has the skinny physique, he doesn't have the attention span to be the coxswain on the seven-man rowing team.

Then, Kip's classmate, Miguel Castillo, was charged with an honor code violation. Cheating by hacking into the Biscayne-Tuttle mainframe and stealing exams in half-a-dozen classes. But Miguel was innocent. Kip told me he'd overheard a couple kids bragging about stealing the tests by first hacking Miguel's computer and using it to access the mainframe. Miguel was the fall guy.

"What should I do, Uncle Jake?"

"Tell the truth. Stand up for your friend."

"I barely know Miguel. And those two guys are on the lacrosse team. They'll beat the crud out of me."

I told Kip to bring Miguel to the house for some of Granny's deep-fried chicken, collard greens, and sweet potato pie. The kid was one of the boarding students at Biscayne-Tuttle, so he was happy to join us for home cooking. Sitting on the back porch sipping lemonade – mine spiked with Jack Daniels – we talked it over. Miguel was afraid to tell his father about his upcoming disciplinary hearing. No problem. He was allowed to have an adult representative present, and I volunteered. Kip would be the star witness, and I'd cross-examine the lying lacrosse louches. If we won, no need to tell Miguel's old man, who was a Colombian billionaire with interests in coffee, cell-phone companies, and airlines.

For once, everything went according to plan. In the middle of the hearing, the preppy athletes confessed and apologized to Miguel. We celebrated with churrasco and sweet plantains at a Nicaraguan steak house, and I thought that was the end of the matter. Two weeks later, three black Escalades with tinted windows pulled onto Kumquat from Douglas Road. The first one stopped under the Chinaberry tree in front of my house. It was a Saturday morning, I was sweeping up the red berries. Birds eat them, then fly drunkenly in circles, splatting against my windows.

The driver, a small, wiry man in a dark suit and tie, asked if I was Jake Lassiter. I didn't deny the charge. He signaled to the second Escalade, and a small handsome man in a beige suit and Panama hat stepped out and walked toward me. He bowed formally and introduced himself as Carlos Castillo.

"Mr. Lassiter, you never told me about the favor you did for my son."

"I'd promised to keep it between the two of us."

"Then how would you be paid?"

"Justice was done. Your boy and my nephew became friends. No need to be paid for that."

"What kind of a lawyer are you?" Puzzled, he looked toward my old coral rock house with the metal roof. The place screamed "Florida Cracker," and must have answered his question. "You'll be hearing from the C.F.O. of my real estate ventures. I have some work for you."

"I'm a trial lawyer, Mr. Castillo."

"So?"

"I appreciate the gesture, but I don't know anything about real estate."

He gave me a smile that wrinkled his trim little mustache. "Then learn, Mr. Lassiter. How difficult could it be?"

He was right. Especially when you hire drone lawyers and experienced paralegals to do all the work. Castillo was flush with cash from his South American operations. Florida real estate was in the toilet. He pumped millions into Miami-Dade and Broward counties, buying up distressed condo developments, working out deals with lenders to take over troubled shopping centers and office buildings.

Soon, I had a nine-person staff closing condo sales and leasing commercial space, and the cash flow was, well…a raging torrent. Historically, in my trial practice, I'm always scrambling for the next retainer, so this was fresh and exciting as hell. A cash cow with udders the size of Lake Okeechobee. The legal work was mundane and repetitious, but so what? I didn't have to do it.

From the beginning, Granny didn't like my new client. To her, the word "Colombian" was synonymous with "drug dealer."

"You're washing his laundry," she told me.

"What?"

"Money laundering. Can't you see it?"

"There's no evidence of that." Sounding very much like a lawyer.

Castillo's accounts were in constant flux. Money flowed in to buy failing properties. Money flowed out to fix up and maintain. Money came back in when sales were completed and leases signed. Hundreds of thousands or more each month, back-and-forth to banks in Central and South America. My bookkeeper wasn't up to the job, so Pamela suggested that, for a fee, Great Southern would handle the work, which she would oversee.

Why not?

One less headache for me.

Pam had organizational skills I lacked. We had grown close. I was sleeping with her, spending all my spare time with her. And trusting her. Looking back, it would appear I'd been what Granny would call a *dang fool.*

ぐ

After breakfast, I headed into the nook I call my home office. It has a small window looking

54

over the backyard, where a couple young mangoes on a gnarly tree were just starting to ripen and attract flies. I turned on the computer, intending to type up a timeline. Everything I could remember of last night from the time we got back to the hotel until I was nearly washed out to sea by the incoming tide.

Settling into the chair, I loosened my pants. Granny was right. I'd put on weight. Too many midnight dinners with Pam, too little exercise. I'd played football at 235, then trimmed down after I'd retired, a euphemism for being placed on waivers and not one team expressing interest in me, unless you count the Saskatchewan Rough Riders of the C.F.L. The money was short, the winters were long, so I stayed in Miami, attended night law school, and passed the Florida Bar exam on the fourth try. If you don't believe me, my certificate hangs on the wall over the toilet. An ex-girlfriend once asked if I intended some symbolism with that bit of interior decorating. Nope, I intended to cover a crack in the plaster.

I attacked the computer keyboard. Trying to remember the details of last night through a tequila mist. Not much in my brain pan but burned out cells. Damn, I was used to having unreliable clients, but I never thought I'd be one.

George Barrios and Emilia Vazquez probably already knew more about my activities last night than I did.

After several fruitless moments, I checked my e-mail. The usual. My appointment schedule for the next week, compiled by my dyslexic assistant Cindy, with more than the usual typos. A reminder from The Florida Bar that I was a couple hundred hours behind in Continuing Legal Education Credits and had better sign up for some classes. And a generous offer from a wealthy Nigerian widow to share her inheritance with me. And then a final one in bold face with an exclamation point, indicating a message of great importance.

From Pamela Baylins.

8

My Pecuniary Purposes

From: pbaylins@great-southern.com
Sent: Sunday, 2:39 a.m., June 9, 2013
To: psmathers@great-southern.com, rmahon@great-southern.com
Cc: jake.lassiter.esq@lassiter-law.com
Subject: Lassiter Law Firm Accounts
This message was sent with high importance!

Phil and Robert:

Within the past few hours, I have learned of discrepancies in various client trust accounts maintained at Great Southern by Jake Lassiter's law office. I strongly suggest that full audits be started Monday morning. In the event that improprieties are determined to have occurred, I will take responsibility for communicating our findings to banking authorities and The Florida Bar. It would appear that I have placed too great a trust in our client and I apologize in advance for any embarrassment that may accrue to the bank. I have made no secret of my personal relationship with Mr. Lassiter, and I regret to say that he has preyed on my emotions for his own pecuniary purposes. I have confronted him with his improprieties, and he has responded with veiled physical threats. Robert, as I fear for my safety, I am asking the general counsel's office to seek a restraining order against Mr. Lassiter on my behalf, as soon as practicable.

Pamela A. Baylins
Vice President, Corporate Banking

9

Suitable for Framing

"…He has preyed on me for his own pecuniary purposes."

What a load of crap! And poorly written crap at that.

But that wasn't what bothered me.

"…He has responded with veiled physical threats."

A lie. A damn lie!

I've never physically abused a woman or threatened to. And the times I found it necessary to threaten a man, there was nothing veiled about it.

Already, my lawyer's brain was calculating the damage that e-mail could do. It would convince Detective Barrios – if he needed any convincing – that I was the prime suspect. I pictured Barrios huddling with Emilia Vazquez, filling in the blanks of their homicide checklist.

Opportunity. Lassiter was alone with the decedent. Check!

Means. Lassiter's belt was the murder weapon. Check!

Motive. The decedent promised to expose Lassiter for stealing, and in response, he threatened to harm her. Checkmate!

I could hear the *clang* of the jail door locking into place. Even without the e-mail, Emilia, a savvy prosecutor if ever there was one, did not seem reluctant to believe that good ole Jake Lassiter – her ex-lover – could be a murderer. And now the e-mail was damning. How difficult would it be for her to believe that my descent was complete? Confronted with evidence of a financial crime, I resorted to violence to prevent disclosure. A good lawyer gone bad, and then worse. That would be the theme of her case. I fought off the sickening feeling that it was a very good case, indeed.

❧

An hour after suffering indigestion from the mixture of Granny's victuals and Pam's vitriol, I was driving across the Rickenbacker Causeway toward Key Biscayne and a meeting with Barry Samchick, my accountant. I had ditched my Bentley, not because of the multiple dents and shattered taillight, but because I felt I had to shed that skin. I peeled the tarp from my old Caddy and enjoyed the throaty, off-key roar as I flew over the rise toward the Key.

I passed the old Seaquarium where I've taken Kip to swim with the dolphins, and we were both splashed by the Killer Whale. I turned left toward Virginia Key Beach, a sandy spit of undeveloped land with a checkered past. Years ago, I learned to windsurf there. Clean, unobstructed winds blew directly onto the beach from the Atlantic, and a coral reef a mile offshore kept the water calm for fast running. Long before then, when Miami was a segregated jerkwater town, Virginia Key was a "Colored Only" beach. Now, it's one of the prettiest natural beaches in the county, even if it is across the street from a sewage plant.

I found Samchick at a ramshackle joint called Jimbo's. The place looked like it was constructed of driftwood, then blown down by a hurricane and put back together by a platoon of blindfolded and drunken Seabees. Two fishermen – old salts tanned the color of rich tea – were buying bait, and the air was filled with the tang of fish being smoked in 55-gallon drums. An abandoned school bus, painted a rainbow of colors, was sinking into the sand. It looked to be someone's home. Three teenage girls in string bikinis that should get them grounded by their parents were trying to play bocce on the clay court, but mostly giggling and dropping the balls on each other's feet.

The day was hot and humid as a dishrag, the June sun peeking in and out of clouds the color of dirty nickels. I found Samchick at an outside table, drinking Dos Equis from the bottle and fiddling with an order of fish croquettes. He was a stocky man with pale arms sticking out of a Hawaiian shirt. I liked him because his numbers always added up and he charged me below-market fees, befitting our long relationship. A manilla folder lay on the table next to his beer.

"Jesus, Jake, I'm sorry about Pam," he greeted me.

I nodded my thanks and gestured toward the folder. "What did you find, Barry?"

"You didn't kill her, did you, Jake?"

Jeez, if my friends weren't sure about me, what were the grand jurors going to believe?

"Aw c'mon. You know better than to ask a damn fool question like that."

He lifted his hands in apology. "Okay, okay. But have you lawyered up?"

"My next stop. Tell me about my trust accounts."

He spent a few moments telling me what I already knew. Every week, hundreds of thousands of dollars flowed through my accounts – in and out – as a result of Carlos Castillo buying and selling properties in South Florida. Blocks of condos, restaurant leases, commercial properties. The man was a money machine, thanks to the coffee industry, or whatever he did in native Colombia.

Okay, I'm not gonna get cute here. I did my due diligence when Castillo – thankful I'd done a solid for his kid – came to me with an open wallet. The man really was the largest grower of coffee outside the big, international conglomerates. His name also popped up occasionally in news accounts as a "suspected" drug trafficker and money launderer. But no charges, much less convictions. In these parts, that's enough to get you the key to the city.

"So what was Pam doing with my accounts?" I asked Samchick.

"Whatever you asked her to do."

"What's that mean?"

"You told her to open an account, she opened it. You told her to close an account and disburse funds, she did that. What *you* did was transfer trust account funds – clients' money – from your accounts at Great Southern to accounts of Novak Global Growth Ltd. in the Caymans."

"Novak Schmo-vak! I got no idea what you're talking about."

"I'm talking millions, Jake. In and out of Novak Global, with money from trust accounts you hold for Carlos Castillo."

"For the love of God, what's Novak Global?"

Samchick hoisted a beer in his plastic cup. "Ah, therein lies a tale."

Samchick told me that Eddie Novak was the hottest investment guru in town, returning profits of 20 to 30 per cent, regardless of how the stock market was doing. A solid education. Harvard, then Wharton School. An investment banker for one of the big firms in New York before moving to Miami and opening his own shop. Now, he was a billionaire who lived high and made millions for some heavy hitters in town. He traded currencies, precious metals, futures, foreign bonds, and other mysterious instruments including derivatives and as far as anyone can tell, magic wands.

In my little world, I didn't know anything about Novak or his funds. Here's how my system worked. I maintained my trust accounts at Great Southern. The money flowed into the accounts, mostly from Castillo's purchases and sales of Florida property. Net proceeds ultimately were wired to various Castillo accounts in several Central and South American countries.

Strictly speaking, I made no money off the trust accounts. Castillo paid fees for my staff handling the due diligence and paperwork that went into the sales and purchases. Those fees, for services rendered, went into my operating account. The trust accounts – dams holding the client's liquid assets – must always be in balance and the funds can't be used for the lawyer's purposes. "Borrowing" from a trust account is akin to stealing, and under the law, it's a disbarable offense.

"From what I can tell," Samchick said, "you skimmed several of Castillo's largest trust accounts."

"The hell I did!"

"We're talking millions."

"You're talking nonsense!"

"You transferred the money to Novak Global, which invested it and returned some hefty profits. You returned the principal to the trust accounts so that no one would suspect anything."

"Barry, what the hell! You've known me for years. Have I ever–"

"Novak deposited your profits into some offshore accounts you created under fictitious names. I can't trace them, but the I.R.S. just might."

"Are you listening to me, Barry?" I motioned for a beer, but it would take more than one to calm me down.

"Well, do you have a better explanation?"

"Sure I do. Pam got my password so she could make the electronic transfers to Novak. To cover her own fraud, she made it appear I was skimming my clients' money. Jesus, Barry, it's simple."

"If that's true, you gotta fix the problem quickly. The Florida Bar is scheduled to audit your accounts in less than a month."

"There's a flaw in her plan," I told Samchick. "Find those offshore accounts where she dumped her profits. Get behind the fictitious names, and you'll find the accounts are hers."

"Good luck with that. Secrecy laws in the Caymans prevent us from following the money out of island accounts and wherever the money is now stashed, there's likely to be equally strong laws."

"This is nuts. She steals from me…"

"Technically, from your client."

"Then sends a self-serving email saying I'm the thief…"

"Quite persuasively."

"And I'm threatening her…"

"And that night, she's killed."

"Framing me from beyond the grave."

I had an eerie, disembodied feeling, as if I were looking down at a poor sap lashed across railroad tracks as a locomotive powered toward him. Then I shook my head at the sheer audacity of Pamela's plan and the tragedy that ended it. Who killed her and why?

"I gotta get a flight to the Caymans before I get indicted."

"Slow down, Jake. Novak's *money* is in the Caymans. He's *here*."

"Miami?"

"Corporate office on Brickell, lives in a penthouse at the Gables Club."

"Then that's where I'm going."

"To do what?"

"Find out what he knows."

"More than likely, he was just a passive recipient of the money."

"In my experience, Barry, billionaires are never passive recipients of anything.

10

The Bull Rhinos

The Gables Club consisted of twin terra cotta towers adjacent to the Coral Gables Waterway. From a high floor, you had a fine view of downtown Miami to the north, a sliver of South Beach to the northeast, the high-rises of Key Biscayne due east on the other side of the Bay, and the few remaining houses-on-pilings known as Stiltsville. You also had dozens – maybe hundreds – of vultures soaring overhead in the updrafts, shitting on the lushly landscaped terraces of Miami's moneyed set.

Valet parkers in natty vests and bow ties scurried across the pavers, gobbling up the pricey German cars lined up at the gate. Turned out Eddie Novak was having a Sunday evening cocktail party, and though I wasn't on the guest list, I had no doubt I could talk my way in.

The lobby of Tower One was all polished marble and fresh flowers, and a helpful attendant pointed the way to the Novak party on the expansive pool deck. The clink of glasses and chatter of people just so happy to be here with equally rich, equally tanned denizens of Gomorrah-by-the-Bay.

An inordinate amount of women were wearing sleeveless dresses, revealing deltoids that rivaled those of LeBron James. Some men wore silk guayaberras, others white linen slacks with buttery leather loafers and colorful Italian pullover shirts.

An efficient young woman with a clipboard met me at a welcoming table. Behind her were two sturdy young men with close-cropped hair and necks bulging out of their white shirts. Security to keep out the hoi-polloi such as my own trespassing self.

I approached the woman with the clipboard. All lawyers get on-the-job training reading upside down, whether in judges' chambers or opposing counsels' offices. They don't teach spying or eavesdropping in law school, but both come naturally after a while.

"Good evening," the young woman cooed, warmly. "And you are…?"

"Warm." I pulled at my collar, giving me a chance to scan the clipboard for upside down, unchecked names. "Peter Bridgeton. Present and accounted for." I smiled at her.

She checked off my name. "And Mrs. Bridgeton?"

Ahh. I hadn't seen the "Mrs." appended to his name like an ankle bracelet.

"Mrs. Bridgeton is playing bridge," I said, realizing I sounded somewhat ridiculous.

The young woman smiled, and I added "Three no trump" for good measure.

ᴇᴏ

The heavily landscaped pool deck was adjacent to the waterway, inky and smooth with the tide running out. I recognized a number of downtown heavy hitters. Lawyers, bankers, brokers, plus the usual society page types. Orange Bowl Committee. Vizcaya Preservation League. Save the Glades. Opera and symphony types who give big bucks for good causes, either out of the pureness of their hearts or to have excuses for the ladies to lay on the pearls and diamonds.

I asked a lawyer I know where I could find Eddie Novak. He gestured to a cluster of people near an outdoor bar. Holding court was a burly man of about fifty. Dark hair with gray wings and sideburns, he wore a pink silk guayaberra with black piping, gray dress slacks and loafers without socks. He said something that made everyone laugh. Either it was very funny or they were just sucking up to him.

I moseyed over. Novak was gesturing with a tumbler filled with ice and what appeared to be bourbon. "Sorry, but the Cayman Fund is closed," he said to his admirers.

A middle-aged man wasn't giving up. "What about Bermuda?"

"Over-subscribed. But the Isle of Man Fund is opening. Just get your money in fast. When it hits two hundred fifty million, I close it down."

"You'll have my check in the morning."

"Mine too," another partygoer said.

"We'll be trading currencies, and I'm predicting a twenty-seven per cent return," Novak said. "Not in writing, though!"

Again, more laughter from the group.

"The S.E.C. would love to shut me down."

"Damn bureaucrats," the first man said, and there were the murmurs of agreement.

I edged into the group and spoke up. "Just what controls do you have in place to make sure your investors are who they say they are?"

Novak's smile melted faster than the ice in his drink. "And you are…?"

"Jake Lassiter."

He blinked. Only once. I extended a hand. Without a choice, he shook, letting me know he had a knuckle-crushing grip. Well then, so do I, a remnant of dragging down a few quarterbacks by the collar and flinging them to the turf while calling them various synonyms of "sissy." We stayed latched onto each other for a couple seconds longer than necessary, a couple of posturing bull rhinos. Letting go, he placed his hand on my elbow and steered me toward a path along the waterway. "Why don't you and I talk privately, Mr. Lassiter?"

When we were out of earshot of the group, he said, "I'm so sorry to hear about Pamela."

"So you knew her?"

"Well, of course. She represented your interests with my Cayman Funds and did quite well for you."

"For herself. I never authorized any investments."

He made a show of putting on a puzzled face. Or maybe it was genuine. I couldn't tell, and I pick juries for a living.

"Surely, Mr. Lassiter, you must know that monies were transferred by wire from your Great Southern accounts directly to Novak Global."

"Pamela stole my password."

"She also had a limited power of attorney from you. It specifically authorized the investments in your name."

"Has to be forged. I never signed any such document."

"Well, that is awkward."

"And illegal."

"Let me be blunt, Mr. Lassiter. The police have been to see me. As I understand it, these were your investments and you're the prime suspect in Pamela's murder."

"The police are full of shit, and for all I know, so are you."

He placed a hand on my forearm and squeezed. It wasn't a tourniquet squeeze, but nonetheless one intended to deliver a message. "Mr. Lassiter, Pamela told me you were stubborn and what was the term she used? 'Pig-headed.' Right now, you need all the friends you can get, and yet you go out of your way to antagonize me. Right here in my home, you are bringing unwanted scrutiny on my funds, and that is very bad for my business. So, I suggest you adjust your tone with me."

As sweetly as I could, I said, "The more I listen to you, the more sure I am that you are seriously full of shit. And take your hand off me before I break several of your bones, a couple of them weight-bearing."

He paused a second or two, letting me know he might or might not let me go, then released his hand. "Do you know Carlos Castillo, Mr. Lassiter?"

"Of course, he's a client. A coffee importer and a real estate investor."

Novak chuckled. If snakes could laugh, that's the sound they would make. "A drug dealer is more like it. The police asked me if I knew the money you invested actually belonged to Castillo. I told them 'no,' which was true. But *you* would have known the source of the money. The police think you were laundering Castillo's money. So even on the off-chance you didn't kill Pamela, they've got you on racketeering and money laundering. You're going down, Lassiter. Hard and far. Long and deep." He smiled at me with what seemed to be sincere satisfaction. "Now, I'm getting back to guests who were actually invited."

11

El Jefe

On the drive home, I pondered just what I knew about Carlos Castillo. Of course, there were rumors. A wealthy Colombian. Sure, maybe he's a coffee baron. And an importer-exporter, too. But some of those exports could very well be, well you know. Or is that just the stereotype, the prejudiced cliche?

What was it, dammit?

Had I closed my eyes to the truth because I wanted the easy money from real estate deals?

I pulled onto Kumquat Avenue, still not having reached a conclusion. That's when I saw the three black Escalades parked in front of my house. Either President Obama was paying me a visit, or my client from Bogota was here.

Six men in dark suits lingered by the Escalades. The security seemed a tad excessive for a coffee baron, even if Starbucks wanted to ace him. I got out of my old Caddy convertible, and nobody drew their weapons. The men nodded to me as I walked toward the front door. I recognized a couple of the thugs from my first meeting with Castillo, and they must have recognized me, too.

I shouldered open the humidity-swollen front door and found my nephew Kip in the living room discussing movies with Carlos Castillo. Kip, an occasional juvenile delinquent but now an A-student, is a movie buff, and at the moment they were discussing the levels of violence in Oliver Stone's "Savages" versus Quentin Tarantino's "Reservoir Dogs." Castillo preferred "Savages," which I could not help but noting was all about the drug trade.

They ignored me a moment before Kip looked up. "Can you believe it, Uncle Jake? Mr. Castillo doesn't like 'Pulp Fiction," and I disagree, like totally."

"Those scenes with the assassins," Castillo said. "Totally unrealistic."

"They're impressionistic," my 14-year-old Truffaut said.

"Oh, I'm sorry, did I break your concentration?" Castillo said quizzically, in an impression of Samuel L. Jackson. "They lost me there."

I smiled a hello at Castillo. "Would you like a drink, Carlos? Granny's been stocking up on Jack Daniels ever since she stopped making her own moonshine."

He smiled and touched a finger to his grey, bristly mustache. "No thank you, Jake. But let's you and I have a little talk."

It seemed to be an evening for little talks. We walked through the kitchen into the small back-yard. A peacock strutted past my ancient oak tree, strutting and squealing…and after a moment, shitting.

"I am very fond of you, Jake," Castillo said in a soft voice.

I gave him an appreciative nod of the head. Maybe I even bowed a little. He was, after all, my biggest client.

"What you did for my Miguel will never be forgotten."

Why did I hear a "but" coming?

"But this thing you have done…" He made a *tut-tut* sound.

"I didn't kill Pamela."

"I don't care whether you did or not."

I gave him my big dumb guy look. It's not much of a stretch.

"You used my trust account funds for a personal investment. You subjected me to the eyes of your law enforcement."

"I didn't."

"My lawyers tell me that my accounts will be subpoenaed by a federal grand jury!" His voice rose for the first time, and his eyes were as cold as a crocodile's.

"It was Pamela! I knew nothing about it."

"So that's why you killed her?"

"I didn't kill her."

He shook his head and seemed to listen to the sounds of the night. Crickets and a far-away horn from Metrorail. The air was warm and moist and smelled of jasmine.

"How did she get control over your accounts?"

I gave the same explanation I'd given to Novak. A stolen password, a forged power of attorney. I added one new fact. "She was also my girlfriend, so I trusted her."

"Idiota! That is even less reason to trust her!"

"I'm sorry, Carlos. I know it looks like I was laundering your money."

"You *were* laundering my money, *tonto!* But through legitimate real estate. That was your job. Not mixing my money up with some private fund that's now tied to a murder. Jesus, don't you see what you've done?"

"All I can say is, I'm sorry. But I didn't do it."

"You're responsible for the actions of the woman. That's the way my superiors see it."

"Your superiors? I thought you were *el jefe.*"

He snorted a laugh. "There's always a bigger boss. Someone far removed from the street. Someone you would never meet. Which is what makes it easier for him to order you killed."

That sucked the wind out of me.

"Take a breath, Jake. I will vouch for you. For now. I'll tell *el jefe* you're a fool with women but you didn't steal from us. But if the flame gets too hot, let me assure you of this, my friend. I will not be the one who gets burned."

12

A Flea-Flicker Lawyer

"I'm not guilty," I said.

"No shit," Willow Marsh replied. "But are you innocent?"

The lady lawyer was asking whether I was technically not guilty because the state couldn't prove its case or was I factually innocent.

"My mistake," I said. "I'm innocent. I didn't kill Pamela but there's a helluva lot of evidence suggesting otherwise."

"Starting with that suck-ass email."

Willow Marsh, my newly retained lawyer, looked like a former runway model and talked like a tough-guy trial lawyer. She'd played varsity volleyball at Stanford where she earned Phi Beta Kappa, and in her spare time, competed for Miss California, finishing first runner-up. Best I knew, that was the last time she didn't win whatever competition came her way.

Sitting in her high-rise office on Third Avenue near the federal courthouse, she was scowling as she read and re-read Pamela's e-mail, the one accusing me of stealing from my clients, threatening her, and causing the explosion of the Hindenburg.

"The last words ever heard from Pamela Baylins," Willow Marsh mused. "And, the last words the jury will likely hear from the prosecutor." She gave her voice a little sing-song quality, meant to imitate Emilia Vazquez in closing argument. "Ladies and gentlemen of the jury, you can sense Pamela's fear as she cried out for help, just moments before this man…" Willow pointed at me, lest there be a dim-witted juror who thought she meant the bailiff. "…Jake Lassiter, a former professional athlete with a history of violence, strangled the last breath out of her."

I felt as if the breath had been knocked out of *me.* That was exactly what Emilia Vazquez would say, while regarding me with the look of a chef who has discovered a rat in the larder.

"Are you sure you wouldn't rather prosecute the case?" I asked.

"Oh, I would convict your sorry ass. At the same time, there's no one else in town better equipped to get you off…whether you're factually innocent or merely not guilty."

I hadn't been indicted yet. The state grand jury was still meeting, hearing the evidence, but I knew that Detective Barrios and Prosecutor Vazquez had put together what lawyers call a prima facie case. It wouldn't be long before 23 citizens would sign the "true bill" attesting that a homicide had been committed and that there was probable cause I'd committed it. Thus would start the relentless wheels of the so-called justice system.

"'As I fear for my safety,'" Willow read aloud from the email that had her so aggravated, "'I am asking the general counsel's office to seek a restraining order against Mr. Lassiter as soon as practicable.' Shit!"

"A cover-her-ass document," I said. "I had just accused her of skimming the trust accounts. We argued and she tried to turn the tables on me. I stormed out of the hotel suite and she sent the bullshit email, claiming *she'd* found the discrepancies in the accounts."

"So you say." Willow studied me a moment, either judging my credibility, or sizing me up for prison garb.

I had decided early on that I wanted a female defense lawyer. A no brainer. The victim was a young woman, presumably killed by her lover, a miserable wretch named Jake Lassiter, soon to be confronted with evidence of his violent nature. I needed a female protector to fend off the awesome power of the state. I needed the jury to see her comforting hand on my arm, her presence attesting to my lack of misogynistic rage.

So now, with the grand jury meeting behind closed doors, plotting against me, I delivered my future – or lack thereof – to the capable hands of Willow Hampton Marsh, Esquire, cagey trial lawyer and still a major babe.

Willow had been chief prosecutor in the major crimes division of the state attorney's office and knew the players there. She'd crossed over and become a defense lawyer a dozen years ago. She was a tall, lanky blonde approaching 50 with grace and wit and intelligence.

The times I'd seen Willow in trial, she was utterly at ease in the courtroom. Despite her Mensa I.Q., she never talked down to the jury, and she possessed powerful persuasion skills. Thankfully, unlike the situation with Emilia Vazquez, there was no past between Willow and me.

"I don't know which is the worst fact," she said, "that suck-ass email, *your* belt around Pamela's neck, *your* DNA under her fingernails, or that half the tourists on Miami Beach heard you two squabbling that night."

"I vote for the DNA," I said.

"Right. It's the damn *CSI* effect. Here's the DNA. Slam the jailhouse door."

"The truth is really simple. When we argued in the hotel suite, she came at me and scratched my face. That's where the DNA came from."

"The state will argue Pamela was defending herself against your assault."

"I never laid a hand on her or any other woman."

"Nicely said. If I let you testify, make sure you say that, perhaps with even more righteous indignation. And instead of 'her,' say 'Pamela.' Personalize it. She was the woman you loved."

I decided to practice. "I never laid a hand on Pamela or any other woman!"

"Good. Very good." Willow made a note on a yellow pad then moved on. "Next we have the ludicrous fact that you, a seasoned trial lawyer, talked to the detective and prosecutor without counsel at the crime scene. What the hell was that about?"

"It's what an innocent man does. A true sign of innocence."

"You know better than that. A first-year law student knows better than that. Cops are not your friends. Their job is to make a case against you. Your job is not to make their job easier."

"I didn't say anything incriminating."

"You made jokes! Your lover was dead on the floor and you cracked wise."

"I was nervous."

"Really, is that another sign of innocence?" Before I could answer, she said, "Now, tell me about Emilia Vazquez."

"She's a fine prosecutor."

Willow laughed. "No kidding. What about you and her?"

"We were involved for a while, about 10 years ago. At least I thought we were. Apparently, she thought we were just fuck buddies."

"That's her rationalization," Willow said. "Be-littling the relationship after you dumped her is a defense mechanism against suffering pain."

"I didn't dump her. I just stopped calling."

Another laugh. A fine hearty one, like water tumbling over a falls. "What you don't know about women, Jake, exceeds what you don't know about the law."

Both ends of that statement stung.

"I've won my share of cases," I said defensively.

"Sure you have. You're big and handsome and have presence in the well of the courtroom. You plunge straight ahead, like a fullback into the line. When you try a case, there are always bodies on the floor and broken teacups on the shelf."

"Is that bad?"

"Not at all. You're just not known for subtlety or trick plays. Like the…what's it called when the running back takes the ball then tosses it back to the quarterback who passes it down field."

"The flea flicker."

"You're definitely not a flea-flicker lawyer."

"And you are?"

"I mold myself to the occasion. If a case takes brute strength, I can do that. If trickery is involved, I can do that, too. Whatever it takes, Jake."

I considered the ramifications of what she was saying. A flea-flicker is a lawful play on the foot-ball field, as opposed to say a chop-block. But the word "trickery" in a court of law might have other meanings. Like lying or cheating. Was Willow Marsh saying she'd do anything to win?

"Not sure you're gonna need trickeration to win," I said.

"Why, because you're innocent?"

"Yes, but you don't seem particularly glad to hear it."

"Makes little difference to me, other than certain strategic choices. I'm committed to forcing the state to prove its case, either way. If anything, your innocence makes my job more stressful."

I knew what she meant. No lawyer wants to lose when the client is innocent.

"You have any other suspects for me to point the finger at?" she asked.

I told her about Mitch Crowder, the ex-boyfriend, semi-stalker. Willow said she already knew about him. It was the first thing her private investigator uncovered. Her P.I. was doing a full work-up on Pamela. If she'd been stealing from me – or my clients – there could be others out there. Who knows how many people with grievances there might be?

"There's something else for your P.I. to look into," I said. "The autopsy showed semen in Pamela's vagina. There are none of the usual signs of rape, so…"

"You're wondering who she had sex with before showing up at the hotel to meet you."

"Yeah."

"Who else was she seeing?"

"No one I know about. We'd never discussed being monogamous, but I was. I just figured she was, too.

"Really, you have no clue who she was fucking." Willow's look conveyed the impression I should be wearing a dunce cap.

"No."

"Because my investigator got the video surveillance at her condo. You usually spent Friday and Saturday nights there, right?"

"Yeah. And Pamela usually spent one weeknight at my place. So…"

"Well the guy who spent almost every Sunday night at Pamela's was Eddie Novak."

13

Strangulation by Ligature

"Fracture of the hyoid bone and the thyroid cartilage was pretty well crushed," Doc Charlie Riggs said, reading from the autopsy report. "Whoever did this was strong and angry."

I stayed quiet and sipped at my Grolsch. But the beer couldn't erase the taste of rusty nails as I listened to Doc describe Pamela's excruciating death.

"Hemorrhage at the site of the cartilage fracture," the ex-coroner droned on. Doc Riggs was one of my closest friends and has been helping me – in and out of court – for 20 years. "Traces of dried semen found on her inner thigh. Sperm all dead, poor fellows. Live sperm found in Pamela's genital tract, which doesn't tell us much. Those bad boys can last several days in cervical mucus."

I took another pull on my beer. "DNA?"

"Human." An M.E.'s idea of a joke. "But not yours. And no matches in any of their databases."

"It's Eddie Novak's. The cops will figure that out, if they haven't already, just like Willow did."

I had told Charlie about my meeting with Willow Marsh, and her delivery of the harsh analysis of my case. Now, I was dealing with the realization that, not only was Pamela looting the accounts, she was sleeping around behind my back.

This was lousy news, both personally and legally. It shot down my wounded duck of a theory that a rapist-murderer had broken into the room. I was sure that Emilia Vazquez was already planning her attack.

"It is not necessary that the state prove Mr. Lassiter's motive for murder," she would tell the jury. "But we can point to at least two. He killed Pamela Baylins either to cover up his own crime of stealing from his trust account or out of a jealous rage over her infidelity. Or both."

Charlie and I were sitting at the bar at Scotty's Landing, a waterfront shack next to the marina in Coconut Grove. The city *padres* plan to tear the place down and replace it with a shiny, waterfront mall. Sometimes, I hate progress.

A breeze rippled the bay and kept the temperature manageable, which meant I was sweating droplets and not rivers. A grilled grouper sandwich sat in front of me, but I wasn't hungry. Thirsty yes, hungry, no. I had just written a check for $125,000 to Willow Marsh. A hundred grand retainer plus 25 for costs. Two years ago, I never would have been able to afford her. But now thanks to the cash cow named Carlos Castillo, I'm flush. And, thanks to his business, I had needed a personal banker to handle my gushing accounts. Sometimes, we don't have to look far to find irony in our daily lives.

"Eddie Novak may have no more to do with the murder than you do," Charlie said. "If Pamela was stealing from you – or your clients – and she had access to other bank accounts, it's reasonable to postulate she was stealing from others, too. Clients she wasn't necessarily sleeping with, any of whom might have the motive."

I told Charlie I'd already raised that theory with Willow Marsh, and he nodded approvingly. Teachers always appreciate it when their students turn out not to be dunces.

"Did Pamela take any phone calls when you were with her that day?"

"Calls and texts were mother's milk to her. Her phone rang or chimed about every five minutes, so that's not unusual."

"I assume Ms. Marsh will get her cell phone records."

"Made and received, sure."

And Vazquez will get my records, I knew. Nothing to fear there. My story that my accountant called during dinner would be corroborated both by my phone records and Barry Samchick himself.

"Did Pamela seem upset or frightened after any calls?"

I shook my head. "I'm the only one who upset her by calling her a thief."

"Did Pamela place any calls herself?"

"Not that I recall." A thought came to me then. "At dinner, she said she had to call someone but never did."

"How's that?"

"At the table, after Samchick called me, just when we started arguing, Pam excused herself, saying she had to make a call. But she'd left her cell phone on the table."

"So she came back for it?"

"No. After a couple minutes, she came back, and I asked how she made the call. She said that 'make a call' is girly talk for 'take a pee.' Said she went to the restroom."

"And you didn't think anything of it."

I drained my beer. "I was too wrapped up in what Samchick had just told me."

"Did she walk toward the restroom when she got up from the table?"

I shrugged. "Who can remember?"

"Did she seem flustered or upset when she came back to the table?"

"We just kept arguing and it got more heated. What are you driving at?"

This time, Charlie took a pull on his own beer, a Mexican brand I think tastes like chilled dishwater. "Did she take her purse when she got up from the table?"

"Probably. She always did. But she'd left the phone on the table. So what?"

"Was Pamela shy about bodily functions? Did she always close the bathroom door when she urinated?"

I shook my head. "If you must know, we'd reached the comfort level where we could pee in front of the other person."

"Uh-huh. So there'd be no reason to resort to the euphemism 'make a call.' She could have said 'take a pee,' or even the more decorous, 'visit the loo.'"

"What are you getting at, Charlie? And hurry up and answer, because with the beer and the talk, I gotta pee like a race horse."

"If Pamela said she had to make a call, I'd take her at her word. If she didn't come back to get her cell phone, I'd assume she still made the call, perhaps the last one before she was murdered."

"And just how did she do that?"

"She could have used the phone at the bar. Or she could have had a second phone in her purse. Something prepaid because there were certain calls that she never wanted traceable to her."

"So who'd she call?" I asked.

"Whoever she had to tell about your accusations. A partner in crime, perhaps. A co-conspirator. Or just a friend. Someone who could help her out of the jam."

I gave Charlie a little smile and tipped my beer glass toward him. Sometimes, a student wants to thank his teacher for being so damn smart.

Now Charlie was thinking aloud. "If she bought a prepaid cell phone, she would have paid cash and wouldn't have kept a receipt. It will be very difficult to trace it and pin down who she was calling."

"Unless we come at it from the other end," I said. "I can narrow the time of the call. We'd had a round of drinks. The appetizers hadn't come yet. It was probably just after 9 p.m. We start with Crowder and Novak, get their phone records."

Charlie smiled at me. "Now, you're playing poker with ideas."

That was one of Charlie's old lines. *Lawyering – good lawyering – is like playing poker with ideas.*

"Then we do the same with every number in Pam's contact list," I continued. "Check for calls at the right time from either the restaurant phone or a prepaid cell number."

"How many do you suppose that would be? Pamela's contacts, I mean."

"Hundreds. And if we add to those every number that called her in the last 60 days but might not be in her contacts list, hundreds more."

"Uh-huh."

The magnitude of the task hit me then, and it must have shown on my face.

"Buckle up, Jake. You gotta start somewhere. If you catch a hit, you may just figure out who was conspiring with Pam, who was helping her jiggle your trust accounts, and who had a motive to kill her."

Playing poker with ideas suddenly seemed like trying to fill an inside straight. "And while I'm at it, I'll solve the Black Dahlia murder, find Amelia Earhart, and discover the truth about the shroud of Turin," I said, motioning the waiter for another beer.

14

The Stalker

I am a good lawyer but a lousy client.

Willow Marsh had given me express instructions. "No more investigating on your own. Stay away from Eddie Novak. Stay away from everybody. Anything you say will be repeated in court, and not in a light most favorable to you."

I'd given the same speech to several pro-active clients who just couldn't let me do the work. Now, the cleats were on the other foot, and I finally understood the psychology of the accused.

I gotta do something in my own defense. I am not a potted plant.

After all, it was the great trial lawyer Louis Nizer who once said, "The facts of the case never fly in through the window. They have to be dragged in by the heels."

Which is what brought me to the Iron Asylum, the hard-core muscle gym on South Beach. Its owner was Mitch Crowder, Pam's ex-boyfriend, stalker, and wielder of baseball bats. Several possibilities floated in my brain as I entered the place and heard the familiar *clang* of weights and *grunts* of beefy guys.

There was a chance Crowder was the "dude," as in Some Other Dude Did It.

Even if innocent, Crowder had been stalking Pam. He could be a useful witness. If he'd been surveilling Pam, what did he see? What did he hear? What did he know about her involvement with Eddie Novak? There was the very real possibility that the lunkhead Crowder knew far more about Pam than I did. That thought pissed me off at my late girlfriend…banker…cuckold maker.

The gym smelled of sweat, hand chalk, and metal. Kelly Clarkson was singing *What Doesn't Kill You* through speakers in the ceiling. I recognized a couple off-duty Miami Beach cops doing curls with ridiculously heavy dumb bells. "Curls for the girls," the Penn State strength coach used to say, belittling guys who were more body builders than athletes.

I saw Crowder, in a muscle t-shirt, standing at a nearby bench press where an enormous young man with a watermelon belly seemed to be lifting 500 pounds or so. Hands resting lightly on the bar, Crowder was spotting and encouraging.

"Six! You got it Yuri," Crowder yelled.

I waited until Yuri blasted four more reps, his face turning crimson. He dropped the bar back on the rack, coughed, farted, and thanked Crowder for his help.

"Can we talk?" I said.

Crowder turned. His smile turned downward when he saw me, and I swear his pecs danced under his muscle tee. "The fuck you want?"

"To find who killed Pam."

"Try looking in the mirror."

"You're the one who was stalking her, big guy."

"I'm the one who tried to protect her."

"From what?"

"If you cared more about her, you'd know what she was mixed up in."

"So tell me. Look, I cared for Pam. A lot. I thought she was trustworthy and it turned out I was wrong."

He snickered. "You thought she was your girlfriend, too. You didn't know she was fucking Eddie Novak, did you?"

"Not until yesterday."

He smiled with pleasure, enjoying my pain. "Novak used to come over to her place nearly every Sunday night."

"So I've been told."

Crowder looked at me as if trying to decide whether to go on. There's a natural instinct that makes people want to show how much they know. Part of Crowder didn't want to help me, but part of him wanted to demonstrate just how smart he was. I waited a moment, listening to The Black Keys singing *Lonely Boy.*

"Then there was the last Sunday night," he said, "the week before Pam was killed."

"Yeah?"

He paused again, as if not knowing whether to keep going. After a moment, Crowder said, "Novak came over to her condo about 11 p.m. Parked his Maserati in a handicapped space, like always, then rang her from the security phone at the front door." He allowed himself a little smile. "But she wouldn't buzz him in."

"And you know this because…?"

"I was sitting in my truck across the street." He shrugged. "I do it sometime. I don't bother her. Anyway, I could tell from his body language Pam had shot him down. Novak slammed the phone down, stomped back to his Maserati, and peeled rubber getting out of there."

I thought back to that Sunday night. I'd spent the evening with nephew Kip. We were bowling at the old lanes on Bird Road, west of the Palmetto Expressway.

"Maybe Pam had another man in her condo that night," I suggested.

"My first thought, exactly. That's why I went inside."

"You have a key?"

"I know the pass code. I went up to the penthouse, jimmied the door to the roof, then climbed down three floors to Pam's balcony."

Nice image. I pictured Crowder doing the same thing at the Fontainebleau, swinging balcony-to-balcony, like an overgrown monkey, finally coming through one of our sliding doors.

"Okay, so now you're a peeper," I said. "What did you see?"

"Pam was in her study, sitting at a desk with her back to the window. Black negligee with red trim. You know the one?"

"That's it? She was sitting at a computer working, and she didn't let Novak come upstairs?"

"That ain't it. After about an hour…"

"An hour! You watched her all that time?"

"Yeah, I got a lot of patience, man. She picked up the phone and dialed."

"I don't suppose you know who."

Another pause.

"The sliding door was cracked open and I could hear through the screen."

"Yeah?"

"She called Novak. Said 'get your ass back over here you son-of-a-bitch. We gotta talk.'"

That didn't sound like Pam to me. But then, I was still learning all these different sides to the woman.

"Did he come back?"

"That's all I'm saying. You're on your own with the rest."

I'm an old hand at dealing with reluctant witnesses and wasn't giving up that easily. "Did you ever see Pam again?"

Silence.

I was doing the math. Six nights after Crowder turned peeper, Pam and I went to dinner, and before daybreak, she would be dead.

"C'mon, Crowder. Help me find out what happened."

"I didn't see her, but I talked to her." So much for his pledge of silence.

"When?"

More thought time, Crowder wrinkling his broad brow. "Okay, I told the cops so I might as well tell you. "When you were having dinner on South Beach, she called me."

So she had made a call after we started arguing. Doc Charlie Riggs had been right about that phony trip to the rest room. But why did Pam call the guy who'd been stalking her?

"What did she say?" I asked.

"You ain't gonna like it."

"Jeez, Crowder. Just tell me. Tell me the same thing you told the cops. They'll have to disclose it in discovery."

"All right, pal. You asked for it. Pam said she was scared."

"Of what? The escargot?"

"Of you, man."

"Bullshit."

"It's the truth. She said, 'Mitch, I'm freaking out. I caught Jake dipping into client funds, and I think he might kill me.'"

IN THE CIRCUIT COURT OF THE ELEV-
ENTH JUDICIAL CIRCUIT

IN AND FOR MIAMI-DADE COUNTY,
FLORIDA - SPRING TERM 2013

STATE OF FLORIDA
vs.
JACOB LASSITER

MURDER FIRST DEGREE

IN THE NAME AND BY THE AUTHORITY
OF THE STATE OF FLORIDA:

The Grand Jurors of the State of Florida, duly
called, impaneled and sworn to inquire and true
presentment make in and for the body of the
County of Miami-Dade, upon their oaths, present
that on or about the 9th day of June 2013, within
the County of Miami-Dade, State of Florida, JA-
COB LASSITER did unlawfully and feloniously
kill a human being, to wit: PAMELA BAYLINS,
from a premeditated design to effect the death of
the person killed by strangling, the said PAMELA

BAYLINS, in violation of Section 782.04(1)(a(1), Florida Statutes, to the evil example of all others in like cases offending and against the peace and dignity of the State of Florida.

Five months later…

15

De-Selecting the Jury

I was scared. Didn't sleep last night. Tossed my cookies – coffee and oatmeal – this morning. Now, sitting at the defense table, I could feel rivulets of sweat running down my back, and yet I was chilled in the meat-locker air conditioning.

Dread filled me, heavy as cold mud. In this very building, I have personally witnessed acts of ignorance, intolerance, and injustice on a nearly daily basis for two decades. Today, I felt out of control and helpless, my fate to be determined by a dozen strangers of dubious intellect.

As ill-at-ease as I was, my lawyer seemed as comfortable as a queen in her castle. I always tell young defense lawyers to act as if they owned the courtroom. All others, even the judge and prosecutor, were just invited guests. At this moment, the courtroom belonged to Willow Marsh. She was on her feet, tall and elegant, in front of the jury box.

"Ladies and gentlemen, my name is Willow Marsh, and I have the great privilege of representing Jake Lassiter, the man seated here at the table."

A great privilege, indeed.

The subtext of the opening line of Willow's *voir dire* was clear. *I'm an attractive, intelligent lawyer, and if I like my client, so should you yahoos in the jury box.*

My counselor went on: "My client grew up just down U.S. 1 in Key Largo and was a star football player at Coral Shores High School in Islamorada. Without a scholarship, he walked on to the football team at Penn State where he eventually became a starter. Without being drafted, he signed with the Miami Dolphins as a free agent linebacker, where he was not a star, but he made the most of his abilities with hard work, dedication and perseverance."

Thankfully, no mention of the time I recovered a fumble, got turned around and scored for the other team…the hated New York Jets.

"Surprising many people, he attended night law school and passed the bar exam…"

On my fourth try.

"As a lawyer, he applies the same hard work and discipline as he did on the football field. Above all he is an ethical lawyer."

When the occasion calls for it, that's true.

"Now, do any of you know Mr. Lassiter…?"

We de-selected a jury in two-and-a-half days.

That's right. You don't select a jury. A bunch of people show up in court – most of them unwillingly – and will be seated unless the defense or the state "de-selects" them. Willow's task is to find jurors who can look me in the eye and promise to be the last bastion between the overpowering might of the state and the steel doors at Raiford. Jurors who damn well will presume that I am innocent as a newborn babe as I sit here today, charged with a heinous crime. If they can't, get the hell out of the courtroom!

Voir dire is a French term meaning "to speak the truth." Not that we're looking for a "fair" jury. The defense wants people who distrust government in general and police officers in particular.

"Would you give more weight to the testimony of a police officer than an ordinary citizen?"

Who's my model juror? A man who had been unjustly charged with a crime after police officers lied to get a search warrant, then broke down his door and shot his dog. Unfortunately, the state would exercise a peremptory challenge faster than you could say "respectfully excused."

We want skeptics. We want people who are filled with doubts about a myriad of official truths so that they have no trouble finding the defendant not guilty. It's a bit of a high-wire act. While we want people who distrust authority, we need them to give utmost respect to the judge's instruction on reasonable doubt.

"Do you have any difficulty following the requirement of the law that the prosecution must convince

you beyond a reasonable doubt that my client was in fact the person who committed this crime?"

For the record, here's what the judge will tell the jury when all the evidence is in and both sides have rested:

"The defendant has entered a plea of not guilty. This means you must presume the defendant is innocent…"

I love the way that begins.

"The presumption stays with the defendant as to each material allegation through each stage of the trial unless it has been overcome by the evidence to the exclusion of and beyond a reasonable doubt…"

Honestly, how do they ever convict anyone, especially because it takes unanimity? And yet, the conviction rate for murder trials is around 80 per cent. If you add guilty pleas to that number, it's way higher.

"To overcome the defendant's presumption of innocence, the state has the burden or proving the crime was committed and the defendant is the person who committed the crime. The defendant is not required to present evidence or to prove anything…"

I get goosebumps just thinking about the majesty of the legal system…when I'm sitting as the defendant.

"Whenever the words 'reasonable doubt' are used, you must consider the following: A reasonable doubt is not a mere doubt, a speculative, imaginary or forced doubt. Such a doubt must not influence you to return a verdict of not guilty if you have an abiding conviction of guilt…"

Okay, I'm not crazy about that part of the instruction.

"On the other hand, if after carefully considering, comparing and weighing all the evidence, there is not an abiding conviction of guilt, or if having a conviction, it is one which is not stable, but one which wavers and vacillates, then the charge is not proved beyond every reasonable doubt and you must find the defendant not guilty because the doubt is reasonable."

Simple, huh? No, it's tricky as hell. Sometimes, I wonder how juries ever get anything right.

But back to *voir dire*. Willow Marsh was a cagy practitioner, skilled at getting the jurors to talk. Once she got through the boilerplate questions, she eased the prospects into talking about marriages, occupations, children, political beliefs, and what bumper stickers they have on their cars.

A juror with a "Save the Whales" sticker is probably a bit different than one whose car shouts out: "Protected by Smith & Wesson."

During recess, two of Willow's investigators mingled with prospective jurors in the elevators and the lobby restaurant. Not saying a word, but listening, alert to any hint of bias…for or against us.

While in the courtroom, Willow was careful not to be too chummy with Emilia Vazquez. It's difficult to later portray the prosecutor as the voice of evil if you're exchanging smiles at the trial's outset. On the other hand, Willow smiled frequently and warmly at me when the jurors were in the courtroom. The idea was to reinforce the first line of her greeting: if this classy lady lawyer likes the defendant, she must believe he's not a murderer.

Willow assigned to me the task of judging the panel's non-verbal communication. Crossed arms and legs and pursed lips do not make a friendly juror.

After two-and-a-half days, we had a jury. This being a murder trial, we had twelve jurors, instead of six. Our dozen consisted of seven males and five females. Three Anglos, six Hispanics, and three African Americans. Another three unfortunate souls sat as alternates.

As soon as they were sworn and got used to the rocking mechanism of their chairs, the jurors began studying me. What did they see? A big ex-jock with a propensity for anger and violence? Or an honest, law-abiding man who was clueless as to the horrific fate that had befallen his beloved? No way to know but one thing was certain: my freedom rested on the ultimate answer to those questions. I could spend the rest of my life eating bologna sandwiches and exercising in a prison yard, or I could be the wrongfully accused lawyer who would become the subject of sympathetic news accounts.

I wanted to yell at the panel: *"I'm innocent! Can't you see that?"*

But I just sat there, hands folded in front of me, jaw tightly closed, and for the first time in many years, I said a prayer to that big appellate court in the sky.

16

Rational vs. Emotional Murder

In between jury selection and opening statements, I nearly fired my lawyer. Our conversation took place in front of the Justice Building, next to the 250-foot long pink marble pool festooned with fountains. The fountains have been broken and the pool dry for several years. Budget cuts, you know. It was November, and a cooling breeze from the northeast rustled used hot dog wrappers across the patio. Black vultures circled above the building, soaring in the updrafts, while lawyers in Porsches circled the parking lot below. Nah, I'm not drawing any parallels.

"Did you ever play any sexual fetish games with Pamela?" Willow had asked.

"Is that a legal question or just for your own prurient interest?"

"We need to attack premeditation. If you were playing a sex game…cutting off Pamela's oxygen, and it got out of hand…"

She let the sentence hang there, like a pair of handcuffs dangling from a bedpost.

I waited a moment as two uniformed Miami Beach cops headed into the building. "Willow, are you talking about involuntary manslaughter?"

"It is a lesser included offense," she said.

"Except Pamela and I weren't playing sex games. I didn't put the belt around her neck. We were drinking and arguing, accusing each other of theft. She swiped me across the face, and I left. Somebody else came in and killed her."

Willow fiddled with her pen, buying time. It seemed to me that she wanted to take the conversation down a path loaded with minefields.

"We have to face the fact that the state has a strong case," she said at last. "My job is to do anything I can to attack premeditation. You're entitled to jury instructions on the lesser includeds. Second degree murder. Voluntary manslaughter. Involuntary manslaughter."

Of course, I knew all that. Everyone in the country knew it from watching the George Zimmerman trial. He received a jury instruction on manslaughter as well as murder, and then got acquitted of both in the shooting of Trayvon Martin.

"Don't want them!" I thundered. "Don't want some compromise verdict locking me away when I didn't do the crime."

"If you were angry at Pamela, as you admit, and if in the course of an argument you killed her without any planning or intent…"

"I didn't!"

"A killing in the heat of anger could be manslaughter. It's the difference between an emotional and a rational killing."

"Technically, yes. But I've seen the state take an emotional killing and claim that the emotion is the motive that proves premeditation. They get us coming and going."

"To sustain premeditation, the state would have to prove that your emotions didn't interfere with your decision-making process."

"Willow, are you listening to me? We're just jerking off here. I didn't kill Pamela, no matter how rational or emotional the reason might be."

"I have a duty to run through all of this with you. You're in a bind. If the state proves you moved the money from the trust accounts and Pamela found out, you have a rational motive for murder. If we prove Pamela stole the money, you have an emotional motive. If you found out she was cheating on you, there's another emotional motive."

"I get it."

"Do you? Even if you think you know your way around the courthouse, this is different. You're the defendant, and you can't be objective. I can."

"I know what happened, and you don't."

"So who killed Pamela?"

That stopped me for a moment.

"I don't know," I said.

"That's what I thought. Look, I think you were over-charged. For first degree, there has to be time for reflection. There's an intent to kill, some moments to think about it, and the killing itself. I don't think they can prove a careful consideration to kill. But second degree murder is a definite possibility, probably more than 50 percent."

"Great. Just great. If I didn't know better, I'd say you're setting me up for plea negotiations."

She was silent a moment.

"Oh shit, Willow!"

She stayed as quiet as a defendant invoking the Fifth.

"C'mon, what'd they offer?"

"Plead to voluntary manslaughter. Twelve years. With gain time, you serve 10 years and two months. But if you do some good work in prison, maybe help in the law library, teach some classes, after maybe a few years, we'll appeal to the Clemency Board to commute your sentence."

"The Chairman of the Board is the governor, and I didn't vote for him. Plus it's a long shot, even if I was the governor's brother-in-law and chief fund raiser."

"I want you to consider this, Jake."

"I already did. I'm innocent. I won't plead guilty and seek clemency. I didn't commit murder or a lesser included offense. Either I walk out of the courtroom door a free man or they can lock me up for life. And either you defend me with your best shot, or you can take a hike."

17

My Worthless Hide

"Ladies and gentlemen of the jury, you are all here today because on June ninth of this year, that man sitting right there…"

Emilia Vazquez pointed at me with a two-toned lacquered index finger that might as well have been a rapier.

J'accuse!

At the same time, Emilia, dark hair pulled back, all business in a charcoal Chanel suit – its earlier versions having been slung over the elliptical machine in my bedroom – looked me hard in the eyes. She wanted to stare me down, have the jury see me turn away, a sniveling coward. The subtext of her case would doubtless be that only such a gutter snipe of a man could have committed that crime.

"…This man, Jacob Lassiter, whose primary job is defending criminals…"

Ooh, low blow.

"…With malice and premeditation, this man, the defendant Jacob Lassiter, brutally and viciously strangled Pamela Baylins, his girlfriend, his banker, and the woman who was about to blow the whistle on his unethical and illegal conduct."

I was sitting next to the elegant Willow Marsh at the defense table, listening to Emilia, my former lover – or fuck buddy, as she would have it – detail exactly what happened that late night and early morning when Pam was killed and I awoke in a stupor on the beach. We were in a spacious courtroom on the fourth floor of the Justice Building. Behind the judge's bench, blond wood lattice work climbed to the twenty-foot high ceiling.

"As the judge instructed you this morning," Emilia said, "I will now tell you what the evidence will show. When Ms. Marsh stands to speak, she will present a different view. All the state asks is a fair hearing of these charges, the most heinous and serious charges known in the law."

"Objection! Argumentative," Willow sang out, rising out of her chair. Her blonde hair was swept up for the proceedings, revealing tasteful, not-too-large gold hoop earrings.

"Sustained," Judge Marjorie Cohen-Wang said, evenly. "Save the editorializing for closing argument." Her Honor had been on the bench just over a year, having been appointed by the governor, basically by meeting the criteria of gender, campaign contributions, and multiple ethnicities. I had never appeared in front of her. Given my testy relationships with most judges, this was probably a plus.

"Thank you, Your Honor," Emilia said with a slight bow, as if she had won a Chamber of Commerce award, instead of being gently chastised. Part of the lawyer's art is to show confidence in the face of adversity. The defendant's job is to show nothing at all, except perhaps a sliver of humanity.

"In one shattering moment," Emilia went on, "Pamela Baylins' life changed."

The jury waited to hear just what that moment was, and so did I.

"In that moment two things occurred almost simultaneously…"

My curiosity was going crazy. And that, after all, is the trial lawyer's job. Make the courtroom hang on your every word.

"Pamela Baylins told the defendant she knew he had stolen his client's funds and that she would report him to the authorities, and in the same instant, the defendant decided to do whatever it took to keep her quiet. He quarreled viciously with Pamela, as several witnesses will tell you. He threatened her, frightening her so badly that she sent a late-night email to her boss and her employer's chief of security, expressing her concerns. Still, this brave woman could not be dissuaded by threats from the defendant. So, when all his efforts failed, as the forensic evidence will show, the defendant,

Jacob Lassiter brutally killed Pamela. Killed her to keep her quiet. Killed her to suppress the truth. Killed her to save his own hide."

She didn't say "worthless hide," but that's what was implied.

If I had been the defense lawyer instead of the low-life client, I might have objected right about now. Emilia's opening sounded suspiciously like a closing argument. But Willow Marsh was of a different school. She knew that too many objections piss off the jury at the objector, not the objectee. So Willow stayed seated on her trim bottom and I did my best not to squirm in my seat.

"A word of explanation here," Emilia said, in less dramatic tones. "Lawyers hold funds in trust for their clients. Strict laws prohibit the lawyer from tampering with those funds. A lawyer cannot *borrow* money from those accounts and later repay it. A lawyer cannot use those funds for his or her own purposes. But the evidence will show that the defendant ignored those laws. He siphoned off client funds…"

Siphoned. A damn good word, I thought. Painting the lawyer as a sewage line.

A line came to me then, Norman Mailer once saying, "You don't really know a woman until you've met her in court."

Just how well do I know Emilia Vazquez?

Not that well, considering we'd been lovers…
or whatever. How well did I know Pamela Baylins?
Nada. It turns out I knew nothing.

Emilia summarized the evidence to come. The
overheard arguments. The video cameras. The fact
that no room key was used to enter our suite after
I left the hotel in a drunken stupor. Likewise, no
sign of forced entry.

It was a compelling story. Some prosecutors begin their opening statements with the accurate but
ludicrous statement: "Ladies and gentlemen, what
I'm about to tell you is not evidence; it is merely a
roadmap of the case to follow."

The judge has already said that, so there's no
need to remind the jurors of it. Let them think
your words are the most important they'll ever
hear. Grab their attention with a compelling story.
Just be sure you have the evidence to back it up.
Emilia grabbed tight, and she had the evidence,
too.

A prosecutor, I've often said, is a carpenter
building a house, methodically aligning the joints,
deeply driving the nails. A defense lawyer is a van-
dal tearing at the support beams with a crowbar
and spray-painting graffiti on the pristine walls.
There's a flaw in my analogy. A prosecutor can't
order the lumber and concrete blocks and drywall
needed for the job. She is stuck with whatever the
contractor provided, whatever evidence the homi-

cide detectives may have gathered. Those are the cards she's dealt, the evidence she's given. If anything is lacking, she must make up for it with cleverness and guile, of which Emilia had plenty.

Jurors are at their most alert during opening statements. They've learned a smidgen about the case in *voir dire*. But now, the juicy facts – or two competing sets of facts – are being unspooled for them. Their curiosity keeps them focused, and the smart prosecutor, the first horse out of the gate, has the advantage.

As Emilia shoveled more and more dirt on me, I began to feel like the miscreant she made me out to be. I wondered if I looked like a murderer. Surely, the case against me was strong, evidence piled upon evidence, inference upon inference. Without thinking, I leaned down and scratched the itchy skin below my ankle monitor. Yeah, I was out on bail, just like O.J. Simpson, Robert Blake, and Phil Spector. Accused murderers, all. I was starting to feel like a celebrity.

Judge Cohen-Wang had set bail at $1.5 million. I put up my house for part of it and paid a 10 per cent premium for the rest, surrendered my passport, and agreed not to leave the county. No dinner in Key Largo, no fishing off Bimini, not that I had any inclination to cross the Gulf Stream just now. But not being permitted, well that restriction on my freedom seemed like a preview of far greater restrictions to come.

The ankle monitor was a constant irritation. In those moments when my mind wandered to some desolate beach on a tropical island, the damn thing would smack my ankle bone and remind me that I was on trial with my freedom at stake.

Conviction of first degree murder meant life without parole. A living death.

"Look at the man sitting there," Emilia commanded the jury, again pointing at me. "Look at his face…"

I felt terribly self-conscious. Was I curling my lips like a silent film villain? Did I have cream cheese on my cheek from my morning bagel?

"That is the last thing Pamela Baylins saw in the early morning hours of June ninth. But not precisely the face you see now. Not the calm demeanor of a man posing for you, sitting at a table with his fingers entwined in front of him. Pamela saw the angry, vicious, terrifying face of the man about to murder her. She saw her death unfold as the defendant slipped a belt around her neck, and with the strength of a former professional football player, squeezed the life out of her with such force as to fracture the bones of her neck. In those final seconds, as the terror and the certainty swept over her, that is what Pamela Baylins saw and felt. And that is the man, the murderer, you see in front of you today."

I couldn't breathe and realized I was holding my breath, likely turning red. Did I look guilty?

Stricken with fear? Why wasn't I ready for this? I was a pro, goddamit!

But this was different. Willow had been right. I'm acting like a client. A defendant. A man whose future is out of his own hands.

I sucked in a breath, all the jurors watching me. On, the looks on their faces. Contempt? Disgust? Hatred? Maybe all three.

What did they already feel in their hearts? Surely not compassion for this hulk of a man, subjected to the prosecutor's rage. That was the word. They likely already felt *rage* with a lust for vengeance rising within them like a poisonous red tide.

Great prosecutors construct their cases like crescendos in music, building in volume, becoming more powerful in tone as the trial progresses. So if this was the starting point, I wondered, just how intense would closing argument be? What names would I be called? What cries for blood would be sounded like a clarion's horn?

18

Three Elements of the Crime

"At least they're not seeking the death penalty," my lawyer Willow Marsh said.

"'Course not. I'm white. And educated. And reasonably wealthy. I'm also accused of killing a cheating girlfriend, which in some quarters is excusable homicide."

"Are you really that cynical?"

I shrugged, something I seldom do, because of a torn rotator cuff from the old days. "Everybody knows the system is biased on grounds of race and class with a whiff of gender bias thrown in."

We were having lunch at a Spanish joint on northwest 12th Avenue, now called Ronald Reagan Avenue, because the former President once ate a Cuban sandwich there. I was also doing a post-mortem on Willow's opening statement.

She had been cool in demeanor, calm in delivery and textbook in style. She reminded the jurors that the state had the burden or proof, that the defense did not have to present a case – though we would – and jurors should not begin to deliberate, much less make up their minds, until all evidence has been heard.

That's important because the state goes first. A defendant doesn't want a dozen know-it-alls turning off their hearing aids once the state rests. There was an alarming study a few years back showing that many jurors don't even wait that long. Many make up their minds at the end of opening statements!

Willow had then moved to the magical phrase "reasonable doubt," the last refuge of the innocent man, or at least one who is "not guilty" in the eyes of the law. She stressed that the state's evidence cannot merely suggest that her saintly client was guilty. It must prove every element of the crime of murder beyond and to the exclusion of every reasonable doubt.

"And the state will fail," Willow predicted, "because the evidence will show that Jake Lassiter, a hard-working and honest lawyer, entrusted his clients' funds to the management and care of Pamela Baylins. It was Ms. Baylins, not Mr. Lassiter, who skimmed those funds in hundreds of unauthorized transactions. It was Mr. Lassiter, not Ms. Baylins, who was going to the state attorney. And it was a third party, not Mr. Lassiter, who killed Ms. Baylins."

Willow explained the "locked door" conundrum. No key card was used to enter the hotel room once I left. Obviously, Pamela opened the door from the inside for a visitor. It could have been a hotel employee or an intruder masquerading as one. It could have been someone she knew. But certainly, the lack of forced entry or key entry did not necessarily point to murder by good old, presumed innocent Jake Lassiter.

Willow then read the jury instruction on murder. That is something more likely to be done in closing argument, after the evidence is in, and just before the jury hears the judge's charges. But just as Emilia had ventured into argument, Willow tiptoed into the law.

"Her Honor will instruct you as follows: 'Before you can find the Defendant guilty of first degree premeditated murder, the state must prove three elements of the crime beyond a reasonable doubt. First, that Pamela Baylins is dead. Second, the death was caused by the criminal act of the defendant. Third, that the killing was premeditated.'"

Willow had paused a moment to let that sink in.

"I suggest to you that the proof will show only that Pamela Baylins is dead. The state will be unable to show beyond and to the exclusion of every reasonable doubt that Jake Lassiter killed Pamela Baylins, and there will be no necessity to determine premeditation. The reason why the state will fall short is simple. Jake did not kill Pamela. He is not merely *not guilty*. He is innocent of these charges."

With that, Willow thanked the jury and sat down. The judge opined that this was a good time for a lunch recess, and that's what brought us to the Cuban joint where I was having a shoe-leather thin palomilla steak covered with onions and a sprinkling of lime. My stomach had settled since the morning session, maybe because I was keeping busy scribbling notes and listening intently to every word the lawyers had uttered in front of the jury.

"You should have told the jury they'd be hearing from me on the witness stand," I said, between bites.

Willow gave me a tolerant smile. She was drinking iced tea and munching a green salad without dressing. Having a green salad at a Cuban joint is like telling Penelope Cruz good-night at the front door, even though she asked you to come upstairs. "We don't promise the jury anything in opening that we can't deliver. You know that, Jake."

"But I want to testify."

"When you hired me, you promised to let me be the lawyer, remember?"

"I've got to testify."

"Jake…"

"Jurors always want to hear from the defendant. If they don't, they're suspicious."

"The judge will instruct—"

"That they can't consider a defendant's failure to testify. Bullshit! Of course they consider it. Juror number three, the lineman for FP&L. He'd be thinking, 'If I was accused of a crime I didn't commit, I'd sure as hell stand up and deny it.'"

"Jake, we'll make the decision on the necessity of your testifying at the conclusion of the state's case. Same as always."

Willow speared a shred of lettuce that might possibly contain five calories. I stuffed my face with an oily fried plantain.

"You must have had confidence in my judgment or you wouldn't have hired me," she said.

"Of course."

"So, will you listen to me, as you promised?"

"Yeah, yeah."

"No more making faces at the prosecutor."

"What are you talking about?"

"During opening, you scowled whenever Emilia Vazquez said something nasty about you. You look mean when you scowl."

"You want me to smile when I'm called a cold-blooded killer. I'll look like Ted Bundy."

"I want you poker faced. Not angry and not amused."

"Okay. Got it."

"And stop making eye contact with juror number five."

"The cute claims adjuster? She likes me."

"You're gonna creep her out. No eye contact except a quick nod to the panel when they come in. Okay?"

"Okay."

"Now, the state's going to start putting in its evidence. Just remember which chair you're sitting in. No squirming. No gestures. No jumping up to yell objections."

"I got it. I got it."

"Good. Anything you want to tell me."

I used my knife to cut a sliver of the steak. "Just this. If you don't let me testify, I'll fire you."

19

A Nephew, a Granny, and a Bottle

I was having a trial prep conference. The participants were nephew Kip, age 14, Granny Lassiter, age 79 or so – no one really knows – and Douglas Macallan, age 20, according to the label on its bottle.

Granny took the position that I probably killed Pamela and wondered whether that was excusable homicide. Kip was reading aloud the inventory of state's exhibits. And Douglas Macallan just rolled down my throat like molten lava flavored with a hint of the highlands.

We were sitting in plastic lawn chairs in the scrubby backyard of my house on Kumquat Avenue. Mosquitoes buzzed, and in the distance, the neighborhood peacocks squawked, an eerie sound that mimicked a woman's screams.

"That bottle blonde provoked you," Granny suggested. "Stole from you and tried to pin the rap on you. You done what any man would have."

"Thanks for giving the state's closing argument, Granny," I said.

"Just saying what you did is excusable. Saw a case like that on *Law & Order SUV*."

"SVU," Kip corrected.

"Self defense is excusable. Revenge is not," I explained.

"Your fingerprints are all over the murder weapon," Kip added, in case I'd forgotten.

"It was my belt. Of course my prints are on it."

Kip thumbed through a file. "Pamela's prints are there, too. That's what the report says."

"So maybe she took off your belt and strangled herself," Granny said.

"She slipped off my belt a bunch of times, but nobody got hurt afterwards."

"You don't have to speak around corners, Uncle Jake," Kip said. "I know you're talking about boning."

I took a long, wet sip of the Scotch and peeked over Kip's shoulder at a file he had just opened. "What's that?"

"Inventory of the trash can at the elevator on your floor."

I hadn't seen it. I remember Willow telling me the cops had recovered the contents of every trash can on my floor plus those cans on the path I had taken on the beach where they eventually found me, face-down, snoozing in the sand. The contents of the beach cans – soda and beer bottles, mustard-stained napkins, a left flip-flop, a bikini top – were the usual detritus of resort life. This wasn't a case where the state was looking for a missing gun or knife, so not a lot of attention was paid to the junk. One item, though, caught my attention now.

One pair latex gloves. Tag number 127, recovered from the waste can at the elevator on my floor.

Whose were they? And did they have anything to do with the case?

"Why would somebody be wearing latex gloves in a hotel room?" I asked.

"Hotel doctor could have paid a visit," Granny speculated.

"Safe sex for germ phobes?" Kip suggested.

"A killer who didn't want to leave prints." Granny again.

"Not a smart killer," I added. "Thin gloves sometimes let prints go straight through to the object being touched."

"But there are no prints on the belt except yours and Pamela's," Kip said, squashing that theory.

I thumbed through the report. The state, ever so thorough when they want to nail you, also screened the gloves themselves for prints. No usable latents were recovered.

"There's one thing they didn't do," I said. "Probably because the gloves seem to have no connection to the crime."

Both nephew and Granny gave me expectant looks. Doug Macallan just rolled around in the glass in my hand.

"DNA," I said. "When you put on tight latex gloves, you leave behind some trace DNA. I'll tell Willow to spend the money to have the gloves tested. It's a long shot, but if anyone turns up with a connection to Pamela or just a repeat felon with a penchant for breaking into hotel rooms, we'll have the strategy to suggest reasonable doubt."

Just then I heard the growl of a car engine coming down the street. Had to be a helluva big engine, the sound carrying behind the house. I heard the vehicle pull to a stop. Someone must have gotten out because I heard a door slam. Then another. Two someones. My little coral rock house has no doorbell. You can pound on the front door or you can use a lineman's shoulder and just shove open the humidity-swollen wood. I heard someone knocking on the door all the way in the backyard. Big fist. I imagined the shoulder wasn't too shabby, either.

Instead of going through the house to answer the door, I wended my way around the corner, figuring I'd rather see my visitors before they saw me. For a reason I couldn't quite explain, I picked up a pair of hedge cutters from a clay pot. Gingerly, I made my way through the dark, staying close to the house, but not close enough to let the jagged coral rocks shred my skin.

When I turned the corner at the front of the house, I heard a rustling, then "Hey!"

I turned in the direction of the sound and caught a fist in the gut. A tight little right hook thrown by someone who put enough hip and shoulder into the punch to hit me hard, squarely in the solar plexus. I dropped the hedge clippers and fell to my knees. I retched but didn't vomit. It took twenty seconds at least to be able to take a full breath.

"Doing some gardening, *amigo*?"

Carlos Castillo, trim and natty in a Panama suit, stood over me. A short, husky man in a dark suit – the right hook artist – was half a step behind, scanning the street.

Not yet able to form an intelligible phrase, I grunted something.

"Those bougainvillea need trimming," Castillo said. "And the red hibiscus…completely wild and undisciplined. Much like you, Jake."

I managed to get to one knee, coughed and sputtered. "What do you want, Carlos?"

"My sources tell me that the state has made you a very attractive offer. One that would avoid the unpleasantness of a trial."

"But not the unpleasantness of prison."

"I thought I had made clear my interest in this matter and the interest of those who are far less agreeable than I."

"Great, have them do my time."

I stood up, and the stocky suit took a step toward me, but Castillo waved him back. "The state has listed me on its witness list," Castillo said. "My testimony is something that cannot happen."

"They're following the money. They need to show that somebody skimmed your dough from my trust account and deposited it with Novak's investment fund."

"My problem, *amigo,* is when the authorities decide to follow the money farther back than that."

"To the coffee plantations, you mean."

Castillo laughed. In the greenish glow of the mercury vapor street light, he looked devilish. "Jake, you and I both know the source of my money is not coffee."

"Not what you told me when you hired me to do all that real estate work."

"Playing stupid doesn't suit you."

I took that as a compliment and waited for what was to come.

"You are worried about prison, my friend."

"Wouldn't you be?"

"A roof over my head. Three meals a day, though admittedly not prime rib and stone crabs. Still…"

"Still? Still what?"

"Must I spell it out for you, Jake? Plead guilty. If the choice is between a cell for a few years or a coffin forever, is there really any choice at all?"

20

The So-Called Justice System

The morning after I had lubricated my trial prep with well-aged Scotch, advice from my kin, and threats from my ex-client, I sat in the gallery of our fourth floor courtroom with my lawyer.

I had a pounding headache and had cut myself shaving.

Willow Marsh looked as if she'd stepped out of the pages of a fashion mag. She wore a designer label skirt and jacket, gray with fine burgundy pin-stripes and a silver silk blouse. She gave me a dubious glance, shrugged her gym-toned shoulders, and said, "DNA from latex gloves? Not a sure thing. A killer dumping the gloves in a waste can is another long shot. DNA matching a serial killer or somebody Pamela knew – longest of long shots."

"Jeez, Willow, could you be a little more supportive. All life is a long shot."

She thought it over a moment, then despite her skepticism, said she'd file a motion to allow DNA testing of the gloves. It would surely be granted. Judges like clean records. If I were to be convicted, the denial of such a motion could be used to reverse the verdict, an embarrassment for Judge Cohen-Wang, and more work, too, as she'd have to hear the case a second time.

I thanked Willow and pulled out a legal pad to write some notes. I am a lousy client in some respects, but I have an endless supply of suggestions for my counselor.

We were temporarily grounded, waiting for Judge Cohen-Wang to finish her morning motion calendar so the state could start its parade of witnesses against me. The judge's long-time female clerk sat at her own desk immediately in front of the bench, her face hidden by cartons of files. The judge was taking a guilty plea in a minor drug case, asking the defendant if he understood he was giving up the joyous benefits of a jury trial.

A sign hung above the judge's bench. "We Who Labor Here Seek Only the Truth."

Jeez, they ought to arrest the judge for false advertising. I've said it before, and I'll say it again. There ought to be a footnote. *Subject to the truth being misstated by lying witnesses, overlooked by lazy jurors, and excluded by incompetent judges.*

Or maybe just replace the sign altogether with Dante's warning: "Abandon Hope All Ye Who Enter Here."

After several other questions, the judge stated, "I find the defendant is intelligent, alert, and able to understand the consequences of his plea."

Three amiable lies in one sentence, but that's the justicc system for you. The system strives for certainty and order. But in truth, the courts are an unruly circus with clowns tumbling out of tiny cars, performers flying on the high trapeze, and pickpockets fleecing the unwary rubes.

The Richard E. Gerstein Justice Building is named after a former State Attorney, a tall, imposing one-eyed World War II hero, who fought a mostly losing battle against burgeoning crime in what then was simply called Dade County. He had some shady friends and more than one grand jury tried to pin corruption raps on Gerstein, but nothing ever stuck. Except the name on this teeming beehive of a building, buzzing with felonies and misdemeanors, traffic courts and drug courts, where thousands of cases were heard each year and justice occasionally dispensed.

Earlier, we had traipsed down the corridor, sidestepping prosecutors looking impossibly young. More than half these days are women. They burst out of courtrooms, skinny files in hand, plastic ID badges around their necks, shouting out the names of cops scheduled to testify. Never having time to prepare, never meeting their witnesses before the morning of trial.

Families of defendants slouched in the corridor, too, anxious to catch a word with their kin. Corrections officers led prisoners from the bridge that connected the jail to the Justice Building's fourth floor. The prisoners, handcuffed and wearing flimsy orange jumpsuits and flip-flops, shuffled across the corridor into waiting holding cells, rank with the sweat of those who came before. The stench of fear permeated the building, which itself was the sclerotic heart of the so-called Justice System.

Drug crimes and robberies were the meat and potatoes of this building just as various frauds – Medicare scams, identity theft, Ponzi schemes – were the main courses of the much more civilized federal courthouse downtown.

Here, too, were murders trials, heard in this 50-year-old fortress along the Miami River. For what it's worth, Florida leads the nation in defendants sentenced to death.

Take that, Texas!

There was a time not long ago when crime was so rampant hereabouts that funny guy Dave Barry cracked that, "In Miami, murder is a misdemeanor." Jokes aside, it is the murder trial that brings the justice system into the sharpest focus. Emotions are hotter, stakes are higher, and if you are the one whose sweaty palms grip the chair at the defense table, then let me tell you that your life is filled with sheer terror.

Last night, my sleep was interrupted by a storm, the thunderclaps awakening me from a nightmare filled with far worse sounds: steel cell doors *clang-*

ing shut, one after another, each door sealing me deeper and deeper into the bowels of a dank prison.

"Before I file the motion to test the gloves," Willow said now, "there's one thing I have to ask."

"Fire away."

"Can you guarantee me there's no chance your DNA will be found on the gloves."

The question hit me hard. My own lawyer thought I might be guilty.

"I didn't wear the gloves," I said, "and I didn't kill Pamela."

That seemed to satisfy her. I was going to tell her about Castillo's threat, but that would only make her come back at me again with the request to consider a guilty plea. This morning, I had checked under the hood of my old Caddy, looking for a bomb, though I'm not sure what one would look like. I took a circuitous route to the Justice Building, and I looked hard both ways before getting out of my car. I figured no one was following me. I was easy enough to find. And strictly speaking, I hadn't turned down Castillo's demand. My last words to him were straight out of a B-picture.

"I'll do what I gotta do, Carlos, and you do what you gotta do."

He muttered something in Spanish that sounded like *comemierda,* which I interpreted literally to mean "shit eater," and that was that for the evening.

Now, just before court was graveled into session, I changed my mind and told Willow about Castillo's threat. After all, if I'd been the lawyer, I'd want my client to come clean with me.

Willow thought about it a moment, then said, "That explains the transactions to bank accounts in Colombia. Pamela wasn't just skimming for her own profits. She was laundering Castillo's money. Running it through your trust account, transferring it to Novak's Global Investments, then transferring the money to shell corporations in Latin America. I'd bet anything those companies are controlled by Castillo."

"He's threatening to whack me, and you make this sound like good news."

"It is. At least it's a red herring that muddies the water."

I was about to point out that Willow had just muddied a pair of clichés, but she kept on rolling. "A Colombian drug dealer adds an element of danger to Pamela's life."

"Castillo had no reason to kill her. She was making money for him."

"Like I said, Jake, it's a red herring."

"That muddies the water," I agreed.

"Anything that complicates the case, any new element of uncertainty adds to reasonable doubt."

"So I should be happy then?"

"Especially if the Colombians make an attempt on your life," my lawyer counseled.

21

Scratching for Justice

Trial lawyers are advised to start strong and finish strong. Hit the jury with powerful first and last witnesses. Memory is a tricky thing. Some people remember best the first things they hear; others the last. This way, you cover both types.

So, I knew Emilia Vazquez wasn't going to start with a forensic accountant, who would put the jury to sleep with spread-sheets of my trust account ledgers. No, she started the case, just as I would have done, with proof of the first element of the crime: Pamela Baylins was dead.

The proof consisted of photographs of Pamela, strangled, lying on the Fontainebleau suite floor, her swollen tongue sticking out of her mouth at an obscene angle, the testimony of the medical examiner who performed the autopsy, and a few more photographs taken in the morgue of neck dissections. All in all, a pretty unpleasant morning.

"There are four manners of death," said Medical Examiner Henry Kornish for perhaps the thousandth time in his career. He'd been trained by my old pal Doc Charlie Riggs to be fair and impartial, which not all M.E.'s are. "Accident, suicide, natural, and homicide."

"And in this case, Dr. Kornish?" asked Emilia Vazquez.

"Homicide by throttling. What is commonly called strangulation. Here, strangulation by ligature."

Emilia handed the M.E. state's exhibit 17, a man's black dress belt. My belt. Size 38. The murder weapon, the doctor agreed. Dr. Kornish was in his sixties, nearly bald with white tufts of hair above his ears. As he told the jury when being qualified as an expert, he had degrees from Yale and Harvard Medical School, and a variety of residencies and fellowships at places like Mass General and Jackson Memorial in Miami. Over the years, he'd performed thousands of autopsies. He really couldn't keep count.

Emilia got down to the case of *State vs. Lassiter*, and the doctor droned on for a while about hemorrhages in the subcutaneous tissues and fractures to both the thyroid cartilage and hyoid bones, indicating quite a forceful strangulation. Implying a big and strong assailant. Three of the jurors looked at me, and I tried to seem smaller than my hulking self. There was some talk about pinpoint hemorrhages called Tardieu's spots on Pamela's eyelids, and unfortunately, the judge let into evidence even more photos to demonstrate that gruesome phenomenon of strangulation.

More damaging, though not surprising, was the testimony about my DNA being found under Pamela's fingernails, which matched up nicely with those scratch marks on my cheeks, gotten into evidence by way of police photographs.

Then there was the puzzling matter of intact sperm cells being found in Pamela's vagina. DNA testing of the sperm and seminal fluid ruled me out as the sex partner. And the DNA didn't pop up in CODIS, the national database of extremely bad guys.

"The acid phosphatase test determined the time of coitus to be 24 to 36 hours prior to death," Dr. Kornish said.

So who the hell had sex with Pam the day before we checked into the Fontainebleau? Chances are, it had nothing to do with her murder, but unless she was banging a third guy, all indicators pointed to Eddie Novak, investment guru and dickwad.

The M.E. was a professional witness and he got everything right. Still, there were questions that weren't asked by Emilia Vazquez, and that became Willow's job on cross. With a lousy expert and a savvy lawyer, cross exam can lead the witness to the slaughterhouse where his or her reputation will be eviscerated. But when you're faced with an old pro like Dr. Kornish, you take a little, give a little, and hope for a few concessions along the way.

"Dr. Kornish, what was the victim's blood alcohol reading?"

He referred to the toxicology report. "Zero-point-three-one."

"Many times in excess of that permitted to drive a motor vehicle?"

"Nearly four times, yes."

"What are the characteristics of someone with a blood alcohol level in the area of zero-point-three-one?"

"Likely she'd have been in a drunken stupor with severely impaired sensations."

"Conscious or unconscious?"

"Certainly there was the possibility of falling unconscious."

"So it's possible, she was strangled while unconscious?"

"Possible, yes."

"Making the scratches on my client's face totally irrelevant to the strangulation?"

"I suppose so."

"You suppose? Now on direct, you stated that some of my client's DNA was found under the victim's fingernails, correct?"

"Yes."

"Did you read the statement Mr. Lassiter voluntarily gave the police the morning of the murder?"

"He said that he and the victim had what amounted to a spat and that she
raked him across the face with her fingernails."

"Would that be consistent with the finding of my client's DNA under the victim's fingernails?"

"Yes, of course."

"Dr. Kornish, was any of my client's DNA found on the victim's neck?"

"No, Ma'am."

"Or anywhere on the victim's body?"

"No, Ma'am."

"Sometimes, when a person is strangled, you find crescent marks on the victim's neck, correct?"

"Yes. Usually with manual strangulation, but sometimes with a ligature, too."

"Were there any such crescent marks on Pamela Baylins' neck?"

"No."

"Were there bruises?"

"Yes. Some from the belt, some that may have been made by the assailant's fingers."

"Were Mr. Lassiter's fingernails scraped for DNA material?"

"Yes."

"Any of the victim's DNA found?"

"No."

"Earlier you said it was possible Ms. Baylins was unconscious when attacked. I assume it also follows it's possible she was conscious."

"Yes, of course."

"Okay, let's assume that Ms. Baylins, though impaired, was conscious at the time she was strangled."

"If you wish."

"If a person is being strangled, won't she attempt to fight off the ligature?"

"I'm not sure I understand the question."

"Oh, I think you do."

"Objection!" Emilia sang out. "Argumentative."

"Sustained. Next question, counselor."

Willow approached the clerk's table and picked up my belt. She wrapped it around her neck and tightened it slightly. "Your Honor, I'd like Dr. Kornish to step down for a moment."

The judge waved her approval.

"Please stand behind me and place your hands on either end of the belt, Doctor."

The M.E. did as he was told.

"Now, tighten the belt a bit." He looked a little uncomfortable, but maybe deep inside, he'd like to tighten the belt just a bit more than necessary. "If someone was trying to strangle me with this belt, would I swing backwards trying to scratch my assailant's face?"

Willow made a show out of flailing her arms backward, coming nowhere close to the doctor's cheeks.

"Well, I don't know," Dr. Kornish said. "Probably not."

"Wouldn't Pamela in fact attempt to fight off the hands that are literally squeezing the life out of her?"

Willow reached for her neck and grabbed one of the doctor's hands with both of hers. Then like an angry cat, she scratched. "Ouch!" the doctor yelped, letting go.

She'd gone deep, drawing blood.

Ah, what a good lawyer will do for her client!

"Isn't that exactly what Pamela would have done?" Willow said.

"Possibly. She might have."

"Did my client have any scratches on his hands or arms?"

"No."

The M.E. sucked at a bloody knuckle.

"Better get a Band Aid for that." Willow sat down, saying, "No further questions."

22

The Timeline Crimeline

"We win or lose on the timeline," Willow Marsh said.

"I know that," I said.

"If the jury believes you were on the beach between 3 a.m. and 5 a.m. and Pamela was killed during that time, we win. Anything else, we lose."

We stood in the Justice Building parking lot, 50 yards from the Miami River. A freighter steamed east, heading for open water. I imagined some beachy Caribbean island in its future, but not in mine.

"Did you tell me the truth, about when you left the hotel for your beach stroll?"

"Of course I did. As best I can figure, I left the suite between a little before 2 a.m. You've got the hotel video showing me leaving by the poolside doors at 1:57 a.m. What more do you need?"

"And you didn't come back in?"

"Not until the cops brought me back after sunrise. You know as well as I do there's no video of me till then. That's a good fact, right?"

"Before we get to that, I've got some tougher questions for you."

"Jeez, Willow, what's this about? Why the third degree?"

She drew a document from her briefcase and spread it on the hood of her Jaguar. Across the street, a wood stork peg-legged up the river bank and wandered into the middle of North River Drive.

Willow held the document with both hands to keep it from blowing away:

TIMELINE

PROTECTED WORK PRODUCT AND ATTORNEY CLIENT MATERIAL

4:15 p.m.	Jake/Pamela check into Fontainebleau Hotel.
6:05 p.m.	Room service delivers magnum of Champagne and appetizers and order is placed for breakfast the next morning.
7:40 p.m.	Video of Jake/Pamela leaving front doors of hotel, getting in taxi
7:58 p.m.	Arrive at Prime 112 for dinner.

8:21 p.m.	Bartender runs tab, two tequilas for Jake, two Cosmos for Pamela.
8:25 p.m.	Jake/Pamela seated, order another round of drinks.
8:42 p.m.	Jake orders bottle of Cabernet and appetizers.
8:57 p.m.	Accountant Barry Samchick calls Jake re trust account discrepancies.
9:00 to 9:20 p.m.	(Approximate) Server, Diners, Maître de all observe argument at table.
9:21 p.m.	Pamela calls Mitch Crowder, who will testify – subject to hearsay objections – that she said she was afraid Jake might kill her.
9:37 p.m.	Without ordering entrees, Jake pays check. Server reports more arguing over "bank accounts."
9:42 p.m.	Taxi driver transports Jake/Pamela back to hotel, gives statement saying the couple argued the entire way. Remembers Pamela saying, "Don't blame me for your thievery."

10:04 p.m.	Video camera records Jake/Pamela entering hotel. Lip-reading expert signs affidavit to the effect that Pamela said "Fuck you, Jake" on steps.
10:12 p.m.	Guest key card used when Jake/Pamela enter their suite.
11 p.m. to 1 a.m.	Guest in adjoining room reports loud arguing from Jake/Pamela suite.
12:05 a.m.	Suite receives ten-second call on house phone in lobby.
Time Uncertain:	Eleven 1½ ounce bottles of various liquors are consumed from the wet bar plus four bottles of beer.
1:57 a.m.	Video camera captures Jake leaving poolside doors on way to beach. Gait is uneven, apparently intoxicated.
2:27 a.m.	Jake's laptop is accessed and opened to Barry Samchick's email.

2:39 a.m.	Pamela writes email on her laptop to bank president and security chief, accusing Jake of financial misconduct and asserting her fear of him.
3:00 a.m. to 5:00 a.m.	Medical Examiner's approximate calculation of time of Pamela's death.
6:12 a.m.	Beach Patrol awakens Jake on Beach.

I skimmed the document. I'd seen it before but Willow had kept adding to it. Whenever a new piece of evidence was locked down – by either the state or the defense – Willow amended the timeline to approximate the order of proof.

A quick look and everything seemed fine. Except two things were new. "What's this 10-second call from the lobby just after midnight?"

"Do you remember it?"

I searched my memory. "Yeah, I answered the phone. Pam was screaming so loud, I couldn't hear anyone on the other end. After I shouted 'hello' a couple times, they hung up. That's gotta be the 10 second call."

Willow shrugged. It could mean something or nothing. Someone could have wanted to know if we were in the room. Or it could have been a wrong number.

"What the hell is this at 2:27 a.m.?" I asked. "I wasn't using my laptop. I was conked out on the beach."

"We just got your laptop back from the state. Their expert determined that someone was looking at Samchick's emails to you from earlier that evening. I had my people check it out, and they confirm it."

"Well, isn't it obvious? My laptop was in the suite. Pam was in the suite. I was on the beach. I'd told her what Samchick told me on the phone and said he was emailing the details later. She wanted to see what he had found, try to assess what Samchick could pin on her."

"So Pam accessed your laptop?"

"Like I said, it's obvious."

"Your laptop is not password protected?"

"Of course it is. I have tons of attorney-client material on there."

"Then you must have given the password to Pamela."

The wood stork had found a half-full bag of Fritos on the pavement and was enjoying a snack. I was not enjoying anything.

I shook my head. "Pam didn't have the password. No one did but me."

"So you can see what the state will argue."

"That I came back to the hotel after a short breath of air on the beach. That I read the emails from Samchick and realized Pam could put me away for misappropriating client funds. That I calmly and rationally decided – hence premeditation and first degree – to strangle Pamela to shut her up. Then I left again, trying to establish an alibi by sleeping on the beach."

"That's pretty much it."

"So where's the video of my coming back into the hotel to commit murder. Then going back out again? Last time I was seen, I was staggering out at 1:57 a.m. to take my constitutional on the beach."

"The state will say you wandered around the side of the hotel to the 24-hour loading dock. They had several fish and bakery deliveries that night with doors opening and closing. Plus, no video cameras. The unions won't permit it."

"Pretty damn smart for a drunken half-assed lawyer."

"Or just lucky. No key card was used to enter the room after you left. The state will say you knocked on the door…"

"Or rang the bell. The suite has a doorbell."

"And Pam let you in."

"She wouldn't have. Not after the row we had."

"Okay, if you have another idea…"

In the river, a rustbucket freighter sounded its horn. In the parking lot, the wood stork gathered itself, flapped its wings, and awkwardly took to the air.

"Try this on for size, Willow. Our suite had two floors. I don't know how many rooms."

"So…?"

"Either someone was already there when we got back from the restaurant. Or Pam let someone into the suite after I left."

"Who? Why?"

"Someone good with computers. I'd told her Samchick was emailing me. She just had to see what, if anything, he had on her. So she asks a guy to hack my computer."

"And he kills her? That makes no sense."

"But at least it places someone in the suite after I left."

"And this guy is…?"

"The witness you're cross examining today."

23

The Peeper

Mitch Crowder's job on direct exam was to tote a pail of water without spilling it. Nothing fancy. No surprises. Just get across one salient point. Pamela called him from the restaurant the night of her murder, expressing the fear that I might kill her.

The state had only two problems. The statement was hearsay, and Crowder was a tarnished witness. If Emilia did her job, she could squeeze the testimony through the eye of the needle called a "hearsay exception." If Willow did her job, Crowder would look like a rejected suitor and stalker maniac with as much motive to kill Pamela as yours truly, the saintly defendant. So going into today's testimony, I was hoping for a draw, which in the criminal system, is a win for the defendant.

Crowder wore a friendly brown sport coat and an open collared shirt that did little to hide his bulk but nicely disguised the serpent tattoo running up his right arm. After he was sworn and gave his name, Emilia did what a smart prosecutor always does. She hung a lantern on her witness's weakness before the defense had a chance to do it on cross.

"Let's get right to it, Mr. Crowder, you have had some problems with the law in your distant past, correct?"

Distant past. Nice touch, Emilia.

"I was a hell raiser, sure."

"Did you at one time work as a bouncer in a South Beach club?"

"Paranoia. Worked part-time when I was 20. Maybe 21."

"Ever get into any physical altercations with drunk or boisterous patrons?"

"Comes with the territory."

"So that's a yes?"

"Yes, ma'am."

The jurors were seeing Crowder on his best behavior. He'd never swung a baseball bat at their heads the way he did at me.

"Have you ever been convicted of a felony, Mr. Crowder?"

Ah, there we were. The question, that if answered properly, foreclosed the defense from any inquiry into the witness's past indiscretions with the law.

"Assault and battery."

Whoops. The proper answer would have been a

simple *yes*. And Crowder wasn't finished.

"But it wasn't my fault," he added.

Emilia forced a tight, little smile. All she wanted was that "yes" with no side dishes. That would have closed the door. Emilia must have prepped Crowder, but it's funny how witnesses sometimes get all flustered once the spotlight is shining on them. Often, they say too much. Naming the crime and adding the semi-denial opened the barn door, and soon, it would be Willow's job to chase the horses out.

Emilia cut to the heart of the matter. "On Saturday, June 8, did you have a phone conversation with the decedent, Pamela Baylins?"

"She called me, yes."

"When did that call take place?"

"Between 9 and 9:30. At night. She was at Prime 112, a fancy restaurant on South Beach."

Next to me, Willow tensed, drumming a pencil on the table.

"What was Pamela's state of mind when she spoke to you?"

"Objection!" Willow leapt to her feet like a cheetah about to pounce on a gazelle. "Calls for speculation."

"Sustained," the judge ruled.

"I'll re-phrase. What was the tone of Pamela's voice?"

"Loud. But then, it was noisy in the restaurant."

"Did she sound frightened?"

"Objection, leading." Willow was still standing. The visual cue told the jurors that this entire line of questioning was a minefield.

"Sustained."

"How did Pamela sound?"

"Frightened." Even muscle-bound Crowder could take a hint.

"Objection and motion to strike. There's no predicate that the witness is familiar with the decedent's various tones of voice."

"I'm going to allow that question," the judge said. "Fear. Happiness. Excitement. Those sorts of things are within common perception."

"So Pamela sounded frightened?" Emilia taking a victory lap with that one.

"Yeah, she sounded damn scared."

"And what did she say to you in this loud, frightened voice?"

Bingo. The payoff.

"Objection, Your Honor. Classic hearsay."

"Excited utterance exception," Emilia fired back.

Judge Cohen-Wang chewed that over a moment. It was a close call. Some judges are "let-it-all-in" and some are "keep-a-lot-out" on evidentiary issues. Our judge was middle of the road, and I didn't know how she would rule.

The statute only gives partial guidance, creating an exception to the hearsay rule when the speaker is "under stress of excitement" in reaction to a "startling event." So, testimony that the deceased shouted "Charlie shot me!" would come into evidence. But the statement "Charlie said he loved me" would not.

"The court finds the statement to be within the definition of the excited utterance exception," Judge Cohen-Wang said. "Objection overruled. Mr. Crowder, you may answer the question."

Damn. I knew what was coming and could only hope Willow, who now sat down, would battle back hard on cross.

"Pam was having dinner with Lassiter and she'd gotten away from the table to make the call. She said she was really scared. Said Lassiter was threatening her. Her exact words, best I remember them, were, 'Mitch, I'm freaking out. I caught Jake dipping into client funds, and I think he might kill me.'"

Emilia paused a moment to let that sink in. Then, just in case it wasn't one hundred per cent clear, she repeated, "'I think he might kill me.' Did you understand the 'he' to be Mr. Lassiter, the defendant?"

Technically, a leading question. Technically, objectionable. But there were half a dozen other ways to get the same information into evidence. So Willow kept her bottom glued to the chair.

"That's who Pam was afraid of, yeah." He pointed at me. "Lassiter. Guy sitting right there."

Emilia had gotten what she wanted, but she wasn't finished yet. She still threw a combination left hook/right jab at the bell.

"You're a big man, Mr. Crowder, a weight lifter, correct?"

"I pump some iron, sure."

"And the defendant is a big man, too?"

"Yeah. He goes about 245 or 250, I'd say."

"Does he appear to be in good shape?"

"Maybe about 20 pounds heavier than when he played for the Dolphins, but I wouldn't want him mad at me, if that's what you mean."

A three-bagger. I'm big, I used to hit people for a living, and even massive, ripped Mitch Crowder is afraid of me.

"And Pamela. What was her size?"

"Tall, but thin. About five-nine, maybe 125 pounds."

"About half the weight of the defendant," Emilia said, in case the jurors were weak at math.

"About that."

"Your witness," Emilia said, smiling at Willow the way a barracuda smiles at a mullet.

❧

Willow stayed seated a long moment. She was ready but wanted the big lug to squirm just a bit before she launched into her cross-examination.

When she got to her feet, she gave Crowder what might be called a tolerant smile. You see principals give that look to trouble-prone students.

A lawyer can start cross slowly, letting the witness relax like a patron in a barber chair. A steaming towel of warm, fuzzy questions lulls the witness to sleep, and out comes the straight razor… *whoosh*…to the jugular. Or you can just burst into your role like a gunslinger banging open a saloon's swinging doors. Willow chose to come through the doors firing six-shooters.

"You've been convicted of at least two crimes, correct?" she began.

"Objection!" Emilia was on her feet. "Once the witness admits the crime, any further inquiry is precluded."

"Except Mr. Crowder opened the door on direct by discussing one of the crimes, then virtually denying he committed it," Willow said. "You can't admit a conviction and simultaneously pooh-pooh it."

It was the first time I'd ever heard *pooh-pooh* in a courtroom, and I sort of liked it.

"Ms. Marsh is correct," the judge said. "The door's open, and the defense may inquire."

"You were convicted of both assault and battery and computer fraud, correct?"

"Yeah, true."

"Odd combination, Mr. Crowder. You were both a tough guy and a hacker, correct?"

"In my younger days. Nothing any more."

"You broke a man's jaw in a fight outside Paranoia, correct?"

"He started it."

"Don't they always," Willow said, consulting her notes. "When you were 19, you also committed identity theft, correct?"

"That's what they called the computer fraud."

Willow walked into the well of the courtroom, closer to the witness stand, but not so close as to require court approval. "Now, on direct, you testified that Pamela confided certain fears to you about my client, isn't that right?"

"That's right."

"Just a few hours before she was murdered?"

"Yeah, that night."

"You live on Miami Beach, right?"

"Sure. South Beach."

"Just a few blocks from the Prime 112 restaurant, right?"

"Yeah."

"And Ms. Baylins was an ex-girlfriend of yours?"

"That's right."

"Who you still cared deeply about?"

"Fair enough."

"So why didn't you run right over to the restaurant and protect her?"

Crowder paused, looked toward Emilia, who gave him no help. "Well, Pam didn't ask me, too."

"In fact, you would have been breaking the law if you had gone to the restaurant because Pamela had a restraining order against you?"

That question had jurors exchanging puzzled looks. They wanted to know more.

"Yeah, technically."

"Technically, you stalked her after she broke up with you."

"That's what she told the judge, yeah."

"And the reason she told the judge that was because you refused to stop following her, coming to her place of employment, and calling her dozens of times each day."

"I was going through a bad phase."

"Well apparently, she was afraid of you, too."

"More like I bothered her, I'd say."

"But on the night she was murdered, you expect us to believe that of all the people in the world, Pamela called you to save her from big, strong, dangerous Jake Lassiter?"

"Objection, argumentative," Emilia said, never rising from her chair.

"Overruled," said the judge, "but watch the editorializing, Ms. Marsh."

"It's the truth," Crowder said.

"Even though you couldn't legally do anything about the problem, Pam calls you?"

"She trusted me. Like I told you, that stalking deal was over."

"Really? Isn't it true that up until the time of her death, you still parked across the street from her condo, secretly observing who came in and out?"

Nice work, Willow, using what I told you.

"Her building's on the bay. It's a good place to sit and listen to music."

"What were you listening to on Sunday night, six days before the incident at the restaurant?"

"What do you mean?"

"You were parked outside Pamela's condo that night, weren't you?"

Crowder shot a look at me, doubtless regretting he'd ever opened his mouth.

"I was there. I think Adele was singing the theme from *Skyfall.*"

"And you noticed a man come to the phone and keypad at the front door?"

"Yeah."

"Someone you had seen there before."

"That's right."

"This night, just as in the other nights, did he appear to dial Pamela's number?"

"He did."

"Did Pamela buzz him in?"

"Not this time."

"What happened?"

"He shouted something into the phone, then slammed down the receiver and took off."

"Apparently he was angry?"

"Objection. Calls for a conclusion."

"Overruled."

"Yeah. Steamed."

"Was that man Jake Lassiter?"

"No."

"Who then?"

"Eddie Novak, somebody else she was seeing."

"How often had you seen Mr. Novak there before?"

"Sunday nights mostly. A lot of Sunday nights."

"Did he ever leave angrily before that night, a week before Ms. Baylins was murdered?"

"No. She always let him in before."

"One competitor gone, one to go, was that it, Mr. Crowder?"

"I don't follow you."

"Apparently, after breaking up with you, Pamela was seeing two men. If she broke up with Mr. Novak, only Jake Lassiter stood between you and Pamela."

"I didn't see it that way."

"You didn't want her back?"

"Well…"

"Isn't it true you crawled over railings to Pamela's balcony to spy on her after Mr. Novak left?"

That sent a ripple through the gallery, and the jurors exchanged surprised looks.

"I was worried about her. Maybe Pam was sick. So I got access to her balcony and checked to make sure she was okay."

"Sick? Did you think she had the flu and the best way to help was to violate the Restraining Order and become a Peeping Tom?"

"She wasn't naked or anything. She was sitting in her office, working on the computer."

"Her back to you?"

"Yeah."

"The computer monitor facing you?"

"Yeah."

"What was on the screen?"

It was a question I had failed to ask Crowder. This is why we all need lawyers. Even old courtroom war horses like me don't think of everything.

"All I could make out was the logo of Eddie Novak's company."

"Global Investments."

"That's the one. An eagle clutching some arrows."

"Then what happened?"

"Pam scrolled through a few pages, taking notes by hand on a pad. Then she tossed down the pen, angry like, picked up the phone and made a call."

"To whom?"

"Eddie Novak. Told him to get his ass back there. Angry like."

"Then what happened?"

"About ten minutes later, her phone rang and she buzzed someone in the front door. Couple minutes after that, Eddie Novak came in the apartment. They were having an argument about his business. She said—"

"Objection, hearsay," Emilia said.

"Sustained."

"Without telling us what was said, what did you see happen?"

"Well, they argued for a few minutes. Then, it quieted down and they came into the bedroom. Clothes started coming off, and they apparently were about to have sex. I climbed over the railing and up the balcony to the roof, then came down the fire stairs to the street."

"Sounds like make-up sex?"

"Objection. Calls for a conclusion."

"Sustained. Next question, Ms. Marsh."

The judge shot a look toward the clock on the wall, letting us know she was ready for lunch.

"Just a couple more questions, Your Honor. Did you ever witness Pamela having an argument with Jake Lassiter?"

"No."

"Only with Eddie Novak?"

"That's right."

"The Sunday night before she was killed?"

"That's right."

"And of course you argued with her many times, did you not?"

"Yeah. That's why we broke up."

Willow turned to the judge. "May I have one moment, Your Honor."

The judge nodded, then shot another look at the clock on the wall. Twenty past noon.

Willow whispered to me. "I'm done. You okay?"

"What about Saturday night? Get Crowder to admit he came to the room and hacked my computer."

"He'll deny it. We need the proof first, then we'll call him on our half the case."

"But we have him on the run."

"You're thinking like a client," she whispered. "We have the jury thinking about the mysterious Mr. Novak as a potential killer. Don't give them too much at one time. And let's end on the high note."

I wasn't sure we should let Crowder walk away. Like so much in court, his testimony had been a mixed bag. If the jury believed Pamela telephoned her stalker, they would either believe she was afraid of me or just wanted Crowder to think that. At the same time, Crowder's testimony seemed completely credible that another man – Eddie Novak – was both arguing and having sex with Pam six nights before I argued and did *not* have sex with Pam. Just what the hell was their relationship about? The jury would want to know. I sure as hell did. So many questions and so few answers.

"Counselor?" the judge prodded.

"Just a few more seconds, Your Honor." Willow raised an eyebrow toward me. I thought about it another moment.

The admissions we got from Crowder were fine, but not enough. We needed to place the big galoot in the hotel suite hacking my computer and Eddie Novak in the suite killing Pam. Or vice versa for all I cared. If I were just one of three possible suspects, the term "reasonable doubt" crept to mind. But there was no way we could establish all of that on cross of Crowder, so I nodded my okay to Willow.

Looking at the starving jurors, my lawyer said, "Your Honor, subject to re-calling Mr. Crowder, we have nothing further for him at this time, and we believe this would be a propitious time for lunch recess."

"Excellent idea, Ms. Marsh," the judge said. "I believe the daily special downstairs is lasagna."

24

Follow the Money

The afternoon session went quickly. The judge granted Willow's motion to test the latex gloves for DNA with no objection from the state. Then, the room service waiter who discovered Pam's body testified. He'd been delivering the early breakfast we'd ordered just after checking in the day before. He'd found the door to the suite slightly ajar, and when no one answered the doorbell, he wheeled his cart inside and found Pam, sprawled on the floor, dead. The testimony did give the state an opportunity to introduce more gory photos. Willow objected on the grounds they were unduly gruesome and therefore prejudicial, but the judge, not unexpectedly, allowed the whole batch into evidence.

A fingerprint expert testified that my prints were on the murder weapon. Hardly surprising, since it was my belt. Unfortunately, no one else's prints were on the belt, except Pam's. They could have been there for a while. Or she could have grabbed at the belt while fighting off her attacker.

That ghastly image came to me, Pam using all her strength, a fighting wildcat, even as life was being squeezed out of her. It was a gut-wrenching thought.

So strange, but I still cared for her. The fact that she deceived me, while heartbreaking in one sense, did not ameliorate my horror at her death.

The fingerprint expert's name was Willard Osprey, a fact that seemed to tickle the judge, who restrained a smile when the witness was sworn. The osprey, of course, is the Florida fish hawk, a large, nasty bird of prey. This Osprey was a wisp of a man with milky blue eyes and thinning hair the yellowish tint of a nicotine stain.

On cross examination, Willow got Osprey to admit that my fingerprints were indeed found everywhere in the suite, so there was no big whoop-tee-do that they were on my very own belt.

"You can lift fingerprints from human skin, can you not?" Willow asked.

"Yes, Ma'am," Osprey said, respectfully.

"Did you check for fingerprints on Pamela's neck?"

"Yes, we did."

"Did you find Mr. Lassiter's prints?"

"We didn't find anyone's prints on her neck or anywhere else on her body."

"Wouldn't you have expected to find someone's prints?"

"Unless they were wearing gloves."

"As killers sometimes do, correct?"

"Yes, Ma'am."

"Wouldn't it be far more likely that some third party who entered the room with the intent to kill Ms. Baylins would have been wearing gloves, as opposed to her lover who was sharing the suite with her?"

"I wouldn't know."

"Well, are you aware of any evidence that Mr. Lassiter checked into the hotel on a warm June day wearing gloves?"

"No, Ma'am."

"Were any gloves found on his person or in his effects?"

"Not to my knowledge."

"So the gist of your testimony is that Mr. Lassiter obviously touched his own belt, but there is no evidence he ever put his hands on Ms. Baylins' neck?"

"That would be correct."

"And no evidence that it was Mr. Lassiter who placed the belt around Ms. Baylins' neck?"

"Also correct."

"Nothing further."

The judge recessed early, either because she truly had an emergency hearing in another case, or she wanted to beat the traffic to South Beach for a food and wine festival.

After court, I was driving the old Caddy down Bayshore Drive, headed to see Barry Samchick. The accountant had done a helluva job creating a trust account flow chart showing money in, money out, and money back in again. My largest accounts, by far, belonged to Carlos Castillo. At any given time, he might have twenty to thirty million dollars socked away, awaiting investment or transfer. Or, perhaps laundering.

What Samchick did was follow the money. He'd already told me on the phone how he tracked funds from my trust accounts to Novak Investments, then to Castillo shell corporations in Colombia. What we needed to prove was that Pamela alone was responsible for the skimming. If I could do it while not being whacked by Carlos Castillo, so much the better.

Samchick's office was in a bungalow behind his Mediterranean style home on Bay Heights Drive in the North Grove. I parked my 1984 Eldo next to his red Lamborghini – the low-slung Aventador with the gull-wing doors – in the driveway out front. Business must have been good. Two years ago, he was driving a Prius.

I didn't know if he was in the office or the house. *Until I heard the sobbing.*

It came from the back. I ran around the house, following a path of polished coral rocks and came to the shingled office bungalow. Barry Samchick sat on the front steps, holding his ears, emitting wails and sobs. On the ground were his broken eyeglasses. Nearby, his Rolex was smashed as if someone had stomped on it.

"Barry, what the hell happened?"

He looked at me through wet eyes and gestured with his head toward the open door to the bungalow. The door hung on one hinge, leaning like a drunk holding onto a lamp post. I stepped inside. The one-room office had been tossed. Files scattered. Shelves torn from walls. Samchick's desktop computer was on the floor, its innards opened, hard drive presumably missing. On the floor, a stack of colorful prospectuses for Novak Global Investments, Ltd.

I came back outside and put an arm around the cowering man. "Who did this?"

He shook his head and pointed at his ears. He couldn't hear me.

With palms up, I mouthed the word "Who?"

"Two of them!" he shouted. "Big guys in suits. Black Escalade."

Castillo's men. They wanted Samchick's report. And they wanted to terrorize him.

I pointed at his right ear and mouthed, "What happened?"

He made a motion with both hands clapping onto his ears. "Big bastard!" he shouted. "Boxed my ears. Damn near broke the drums. Said if I testified and mentioned Castillo's name, next time, he'd stick a gun in my ear!"

"I'm sorry, Barry. This is my fault."

"Damn fucking straight!"

"Do you have the documents backed up?"

"Fuck you! I'm not testifying."

I took that to be a "yes." *And* a "fuck you."

"I had every dollar pinned down! From your trust account to Novak Global to Castillo's purchases of gold bullion. Futures market in Chicago. Real estate in Honduras. Even a week at the Ritz Carlton on St. Thomas."

"What do we care about a hotel bill?"

"I don't care! I just thought you would. Carlos Castillo spent the week there with Pamela Baylins."

25

The Floozy

I wasn't drunk exactly, but I wasn't sober either.

I was being consoled by my nephew, criticized by my Granny, and warmed by a tumbler of sour mash whiskey.

"Told you she was a floozy," Granny said for the ninth or tenth time.

"Maybe this can help the case," Kip said.

Glug, glug, glug, Jack Daniels said, a river of liquid gold flowing down the throat.

We were once again on the back porch of my little coral rock house on Kumquat Avenue. Peacocks were screeching while they hunted and pecked for whatever it was the big birds hunted and pecked. Overhead, a flock of green parrots, resembling a squadron of fighter jets, dive bombed the palm trees.

"How, Kip?" I asked. "How can Pam screwing my client help my case?"

"I dunno exactly. But aren't most murders committed by people who know the victims?"

"Yeah, sure. But what's the motive? With me, they've got the allegation about stealing from the trust accounts. With Novak, we can prove they argued. With Crowder, we have the oldest motive in the book, jealousy. But what skin did Castillo have in the game?"

Granny chuckled lasciviously and said, "You really want me to answer that in front of the boy?"

"Which man was she closest to?" Kip asked, ignoring Granny's filthy mind.

"I thought it was me. But Mitch Crowder seems to be the one she called when the going got tough."

"So maybe he can answer the question about Castillo."

I thought about the kid's idea. Crowder had helped before, though hardly willingly.

Now, I had a stack of files in front of me. The trust account records, with all the circuitous transfers of money in and out of Novak Global Investments and all of Pamela's personal brokerage accounts we'd gotten through pre-trial discovery. She had her own investments with Novak and had been making a steady 20 to 30 per cent per year. But on Monday morning, the day after Crowder peeped on the Pam/Novak squabble-cum-fuck, she liquidated all her personal Global accounts and Castillo's clean-as-a-laundry accounts as well.

Why? What did Pam learn that Sunday night?

I tried to re-construct what I knew from Crowder. First, Pam turns Novak away from her condo. She's looking at her computer, the Novak Global Investments logo on the screen. She sees something and calls Novak, who returns to the condo. They argue…then have sex.

None of it made any sense to me. Unless…

A thought came to me. It all had to do with Novak and just how amoral Pam was. And maybe how I'd underestimated Mitch Crowder from the start.

"What are you gonna do, Uncle Jake?" Kip asked.

"Gonna follow your advice. Gonna talk to the guy Pam trusted."

જી

I found Mitch Crowder in the cramped office inside the Iron Asylum on South Beach. Only a few late-night gym rats were still working out. Crowder was wearing nylon shorts and a University of Miami cropped tee. A 16-ounce Budweiser sat on his cluttered desk. Three of its deceased cousins reclined in a metal waste basket. My guess was that we were equally plastered.

"The fuck you want, shyster?"

"That night you crawled up the balcony and spied on Pam…"

He belched a Bud burp. "What about it?"

"In court you didn't tell everything."

"I wasn't asked everything."

"Before Novak came in, you were looking through the window, watching Pam work at the computer."

"What about it?"

"You said you saw the logo of Novak Global."

"I did."

"You left the impression Pam was on the company website."

He took a long gulp of beer. "I never said it was the website."

"I just realized that tonight over some whiskey. So what was she looking at?"

"You tell me, shyster man."

"I have the glimmer of an idea, and if I'm right, you oughta be damn proud of yourself."

"I know your lawyer games. You're trying to get me to talk, to boast about what I did. But you're not getting it out of me, so go the fuck home."

"That night on the computer. Pam was looking at Novak Global's internal documents. Studying them."

Crowder shrugged as if he didn't understand.

"You mislead a lot of people, Crowder, because you look like you have muscles for brains. But as a nerdy kid, you were a terrific hacker, even if you did get busted for identity fraud."

"So?"

"I figure you hacked Novak Global's mainframe or their cloud, or wherever the hell they keep their secrets. You got their internal documents and sent them to Pam. The reason you were on the balcony had nothing to do with Novak. He'd already driven off. You wanted to see what happened when Pam read the financials."

"Novak's financials were public records."

"Oh, sure. The ones that showed him paying incredible returns, even after the stock market crashed and real estate was dead. But I'm talking about the real numbers. Maybe you had a hunch about Global, or maybe you just did it because you hated Novak for screwing Pam. Either way, you didn't bother with the public filings. You hacked Novak's computers to get the real documents."

"And what's my motive for committing a crime like that?"

"To tank Pam's relationship with Novak. And if Pam wasn't such a fucking sociopath, your plan would have worked. Hell, her first reaction was horror. How could Novak have done this? She sent him away. But then, she must have thought about it as she studied the numbers. Maybe she admired that he could pull it off all those years. Her crusty criminal heart envied the son-of-a-bitch. In the end, she wasn't mad at him for being a con artist and a thief. She was mad he hadn't told her! So after berating him, she fucks him. Face it, Crowder, the two of them were made for each other."

"Crazy fucking theory if you ask me."

"I feel bad for you. Deep down, you probably loved Pam more than anyone else. And all you succeeded in doing was driving those two miscreants closer together. All your clever plans and all you got was a little lover's spat."

"You're nuts. I don't know anything about Global. I just run a gym."

"Bullshit. I'd bet anything the documents showed that Eddie Novak's been running a Ponzi scheme. A fraud. A pyramid. A multi-million-dollar scam. That's why Pam closed out her account and Castillo's the next morning. But woe to those suckers who stayed in. They're gonna get slaughtered when this comes out in court. And when it does, you'll be the number one suspect in Pam's murder."

"That's nuts. You just said I loved her."

"But you couldn't get over the fucking unfairness of it all. You drove Pam out of Novak's investments and straight into his bed."

26

The Cornstarch Alibi

I was drinking Cuban coffee outside the Justice Building when Willow Marsh strutted over on those long legs, a smile forming, her eyes flashing. "I've got great news and not-so-great news," she said.

"Let's start with the great."

"What's the best possible piece of evidence we could come up with?"

"We could place someone else in the hotel suite after I left."

"We got it!"

I felt my hopes soar as high as those black vultures over the Justice Building.

"It's Mitch Crowder!" Willow said, triumphantly.

"I knew it!"

"I thought you'd be happy." She signaled the vendor at the coffee wagon for her own nitroglycerine, a/k/a Cuban coffee. "The DNA came back from the gloves. It matches Crowder."

"Wait a second. We can't place the gloves in the room, only in the garbage can next to the elevators."

"The gloves were lubricated with cornstarch. Trace amounts of cornstarch were found on your laptop keys. That's all the nexus we need to the gloves. Crowder was hacking your computer to find Samchick's email."

"That's why Pam called him from the restaurant. Not because she was afraid of me."

"Her histrionics in the suite were intended to get you out of there so Crowder could come up."

"Exactly. She's the one who suggested I go get some air. Then she let Crowder into the room, which explains why no pass key was used." My excitement waned. "But what's not so great?"

"There's no cornstarch on your belt. Or on Pam's neck. Or anywhere on Pam."

"Not good."

"Yeah. It's illogical that Crowder went to a lot of trouble to keep his prints off your computer by wearing gloves but wouldn't care if he left them on Pam's neck."

"But he *didn't* leave any prints."

"No, but think about it. No one takes off their gloves to strangle someone."

"So if Crowder didn't kill her, who did?"

Willow shrugged. "It's a conundrum. We've effectively placed him in the suite and simultaneously ruled him out as a suspect."

"Unless he came in with someone else."

"Who?"

I sipped at my Cuban coffee. Sometimes, the combination of sugar and caffeine will stimulate an idea or two. This time, it only made me jittery.

"Damn, damn, damn," I said. "Does the state have the DNA results, too?"

"And the cornstarch. Everything's shared. You know that. No more trial by ambush." Willow took in enough of her Cuban coffee to make her eyes water.

"What about Eddie Novak?" Willow suggested. "Could he have been with Crowder?"

"Crowder hates him." I told Willow about out inebriated conversation. How Crowder tried to break up the Pam/Novak lovebirds and how it just seemed to bring them closer together.

"Some piece of work, your Pam," Willow said. "She gets turned on because Novak creates a Ponzi scheme that fools the whole city."

"We keep coming back to the same question," I said. "Who had the motive to kill Pam?"

☙

Once they had the glove DNA, the state had a potential problem with Crowder as a witness. Just as before, Emilia Vazquez chose to hang a lantern on the dilemma and turn it into a plus. No way she would rest without confronting head-on the fact that Mitch Crowder was in the hotel suite the night of the murder.

She did this with four witnesses.

A crime scene investigator identified the surgical gloves as having been found in the trash can at the elevators on our floor. He also established chain of custody with a yawn-inducing explanation of the police department's bagging and tagging and storing system.

A DNA expert took two hours to essentially say that deoxyribonucleic acid was the molecule that encodes the genetic instructions of all living organisms. It took another hour to explain how he extracted DNA from the latex surgical gloves and 45 minutes after that to conclude that there was less than one chance in a zillion that the gloves were worn by someone other than Mitch Crowder.

Next, a chemist linked the cornstarch on the surgical gloves to the keys on my computer and declared unequivocally that no cornstarch was found on the murder weapon – my belt – or on Pamela Baylins. Emilia practically crowed at this news. The picture for the jury was becoming clearer. Mitch was there, helping Pam...not killing her.

Next, a computer expert explained that whoever wore the gloves discovered my password by using any of a hundred possible mobile hack tools. Once the password was obtained, at 2:27 a.m., my email was opened to the message sent earlier in the evening from Barry Samchick. The state put the e-mail into evidence, Samchick expressing shock that my trust accounts were out of whack and questioning my integrity. The implication was that I had done something wrong, so already Emilia Vazquez was turning this evidentiary jar of turds into a pot of gold for the state.

Twelve minutes later, at 2:39 a.m., the computer expert said, Pamela used her own laptop to send her frantic e-mail to her boss. That legal gambit allowed Emilia to get this little ditty in front of the jury a second time:

"Within the past few hours, I have learned of discrepancies in various client trust accounts maintained at Great Southern by Jake Lassiter's law office. I strongly suggest that full audits be started Monday morning. In the event that improprieties are determined to have occurred, I will take responsibility for communicating our findings to banking authorities and The Florida Bar.

"It would appear that I have placed too great a trust in our client and I apologize in advance for any embarrassment that may accrue to the bank. I have made no secret of my personal relationship with Mr. Lassiter, and I regret to say that he has preyed on my emotions for his own pecuniary purposes. I have confronted him with his improprieties, and he has responded with veiled physical threats. Robert, as I fear

for my safety, I am asking the general counsel's office to seek a restraining order against Mr. Lassiter on my behalf, as soon as practicable."

It was a bravo performance for the prosecution. Without recalling Crowder to the stand and subjecting him to cross examination, Emilia was able to bolster her case. All in all, a pretty shitty day in court for the good guys.

Finally, as if all that weren't enough, Emilia recalled one of the hotel security managers for one final thrust of the rapier. At precisely 2:39 a.m., the very moment Pamela was writing her I'm-so-scared email – and obviously very much alive – there was Crowder leaving the hotel by the front doors. Alone. The man's alibi was complete, and we were no closer to pointing a finger at some other dude.

Willow kept a poker face in front of the jury while this dagger was being twisted into our guts. Shortly thereafter – we'd worked past 6 p.m. – the judge adjourned for the day. When the jury filed out, Willow forced a smile, but I could see the concern in her eyes. "We'll have better days," she said. It's what lawyers do for their clients, shout out *sis-boom-bah* in the face of impending doom.

"Sure we will," I said. "By the way, if I could have sneaked back through the hotel's delivery entrance, so could Crowder."

"I know. I know. I've thought of that."

"Let me ask you something else, Willow. Here's Mitch Crowder, a guy who can bench press a city bus, and he's in the hotel suite in the middle of the night. If Pamela is so damn scared I'd come back and hurt her, why the hell doesn't she have him stay?"

27

One-Way Ticket

I slid into the front seat of my 1984 Biarritz Eldorado and immediately felt the barrel of a gun pressed against the back of my head.

"Fuck!" was all I could say.

"Relax, Lassiter. I'm your best friend in the world."

I shot a look at the rear-view mirror. Eddie Novak sat in my backseat, his right hand holding what looked like a nine millimeter Glock, his arm jiggling. The barrel scraped at the nape of my neck. I had expected one of Castillo's thugs, so if anything, this was a relief. Except the way Novak's hand was shaking, this could be even more dangerous.

"Novak, I'm guessing you haven't done much of this, so do us both a favor and take your finger off the trigger."

"I'm not here to kill you, but I will if I have to."

"Think hard about it. It's a lot messier than juggling numbers on a profit-and-loss statement."

"Turn on the ignition. We need some air in here. I'm *schvitzing* my ass off."

"Did you fucking jimmy my door lock?" The engine turned over with a cough and sputter, and the A/C came to life. "Do you know how much it costs to repair this old boat?"

"Shut up and listen. I don't think you killed Pam."

"You got a funny way of showing your appreciation."

My eyes flicked to the rear-view mirror. He'd taken off his sleek lightweight sport coat – Zenga, I'd guess – and was sweating through a coral blue shirt. His cuff links were heavy gold nuggets. He looked as if he'd lost weight since I'd seen him at the party at the Gables Club.

"My problem with you has nothing to do with Pam," Novak said. "Crowder tells me you know all about Global's finances."

"Well, aren't you just one happy little family?"

"I pay him to keep quiet, and I can do the same with you."

"How? I'm on trial for my life. Evidence you were running a Ponzi scheme is part of my defense."

"I know that, and so does Carlos Castillo."

"You and Castillo? Perfect."

He blames me for the fuck-up. For Pam finding out and horning her way in. For you and your big mouth. He wants to kill you, but I told him there was a way around it."

"Suddenly, I like you a lot better, Novak. In fact, you're my favorite sleazebag Ponzi schemer."

"Do you know how to get to Tamiami Airport from here?"

"West on the Dolphin Expressway, south on the Turnpike would be my guess. But then I don't own a private jet."

"I do, pal, and this is your lucky day, 'cause you're getting a ride to Rio de Janeiro and a briefcase filled with cash."

"Wait a second. What did you say a minute ago? 'Pam finding out and horning her way in?' What the hell does that mean?"

"Crowder says you figured it out."

"I figured out Pam got all hot and bothered when she found you were running a Ponzi scheme and she couldn't wait to jump your bones."

"That's half the equation, but it leaves something out. C'mon, Lassiter, you've figured Pam out. What makes her tick?"

I thought about it a moment, and then it seemed obvious. "Greed. She extorted you, blackmailed you!"

"She called it a non-disclosure agreement, but that's about it."

"Pam told you she'd blow the whistle on the Ponzi scheme if you didn't cut her in for a piece of the action."

"Finally, you're starting to see our mutual girl-friend through clear eyes."

A police car pulled into a parking spot near us. The lot was crawling with cops. We were, after all, outside the criminal Justice Building. It was not the smartest place to pull a gun on someone. Again, I didn't think Novak had much experience at this. But strangling a blackmailing woman? Maybe he was better at that.

"Jesus, Novak, you just confessed to a motive to kill Pam."

"Only if I believed her. Only if I believed she'd really go to the S.E.C. or U.S. Attorney."

He didn't have to explain. If Pam blew the whistle, she opened herself to scrutiny. Her dipping into my trust accounts would have come out. Plus there was the matter of Carlos Castillo, a guy not as squeamish about bloodshed. Any investigation of Novak Global would soon turn to one of his biggest investors, and Castillo would rightly blame Pam. Still, for my purposes – beating a murder rap – Pam extorting Novak was a helluva good way to distract attention from me to another possible killer.

"Easiest thing for me was to cut Pam in. Hell, I was rolling in cash."

He could be telling the truth, I thought. Or this could be his cover-his-ass story for killing Pam to shut her up.

"My main concern wasn't Pam," Novak said. "It was keeping Carlos Castillo happy."

"He's not gonna be happy with me living the good life in Rio."

"Like I said, he'd prefer you dead. But I told him that you have this weird sense of honor. If you took the money, you'd honor the deal. No testimony. No cooperation with the state or feds."

I thought a moment about Rio. I'd been to Carnaval once. I seemed to remember dancing to a lot of samba music, drinking way too many caipirinhas, and a woman named Gabriela or maybe it was Carolina, or it could have been both. I had the distinct feeling that life on the lam would not be an endless Carnaval. I also thought the plan for delivering me to Brazil might include tossing me out of the plane 30,000 feet above the Atlantic Ocean. Finally, I thought of my nephew Kip and my Granny. So in the end, there was only one possible decision.

"Well, you better shoot me, Novak, because I'm not jumping bail and I'm not going to Rio."

I heard him sigh. Just as he believed Pam wouldn't turn him in, I believed he wouldn't shoot me, at least not in the Justice Building parking lot. When I felt the pressure from the gun barrel drop away, I spun an elbow behind me and caught him flush on the bridge of the nose. He howled, dropped the gun, and both hands went to his face.

I leapt out of the car, opened the back door, and dragged Novak out. He was bleeding all over his blue shirt and my red velvet pillowed upholstery. Grabbing him by his shirt collars, I slammed him over the trunk of the car.

"Did you kill her, you son-of-a-bitch?"

"Nuh, nuh." Blood leaked into his mouth.

"Who did?"

"I always thought it was Crowder. He couldn't stand life without her."

"He's got an alibi. What about Castillo?"

He ran his shirt sleeve under his nose to wipe off the blood. "He was fucking her and making money off her. What's his motive?"

"I don't know yet," I said, "but every hard-on who slept with Pam seemed to have one reason or another to kill her."

28

Me and My Big Mouth

"…Anything you say or do may be used against you in a court of law."

"What happened when you awoke Mr. Lassiter on the beach?" Emilia Vazquez asked.

"He threatened to break my leg," the Beach Patrol hunk said.

"Then what happened?"

"I informed Mr. Lassiter that he was breaching a city ordinance that forbids overnight camping on the beach."

"His reaction?"

"He was uncooperative. Claimed he wasn't camping because he wasn't toasting marshmallows."

If you ask me, it was funnier the way I said it. Never let a cop recite your best lines. Lenny Bruce knew this.

"What happened next?"

"I instructed Mr. Lassiter to get to his feet, and he told me to…quote…go pound sand…close quote. Then he laughed. He seemed to think that was some sort of joke."

"How would you describe Mr. Lassiter's overall demeanor?"

"Objection! Calls for a conclusion," Willow sang out.

"Sustained. Please re-rephrase Ms. Vazquez."

"What was Mr. Lassiter's appearance?"

"Disheveled. He was missing one shoe. The tide was coming in and he was getting wet. Shirt was unbuttoned. His eyes were bloodshot, and he stunk of alcohol and sweat."

We'd never claimed I'd just stepped out of the pages of GQ.

"Was he wearing a belt?"

"No. His pants were drooping, and he was missing a belt."

"You told us about the bloodshot eyes? Anything else about Mr. Lassiter's face?"

"There was a bloody scratch approximately three inches in length across his left cheek. It appeared fresh."

"What happened next, Officer?"

"I told Mr. Lassiter he'd get run over by the half-track that would be clearing seaweed in a few minutes. Basically, I just wanted to help him."

"Move to strike what the witness wanted," Willow shot back.

"Sustained," the judge said. "The jury shall disregard the witness's last sentence."

"Then what happened?"

"Mr. Lassiter grabbed me by the ankle and pulled me to the ground. Then I Tasered him."

Ouch. I remember that.

On cross examination, Mr. Beach Patrol denied kicking me in the ribs, a blatant lie, but the only one who could contradict it was the accused murderer without a belt and with a bloody scratch on his face.

The next witness was Homicide Detective George Barrios, who had testified so many times he was as comfortable on the witness stand as in his Barcalounger at home watching the Miami Heat. Close to 60, bald, alert eyes that had seen it all, he would never lie. The way he put cases together, he didn't have to.

"Did you have a conversation with the defendant in the early morning of June 9 of this year?"

"Yes, I did."

"Where did the conversation take place?"

"In the Sorrento Penthouse of the Fontainebleau Hotel."

"What occasioned this conversation?"

"The Beach Patrol brought Mr. Lassiter to the hotel from where he'd been passed out on the beach. The strangled body of the decedent Pamela Baylins lay on the living room floor of the suite."

"Was Mr. Lassiter under arrest or in custody?"

"No, he was not. He could have left at any time."

In other words it was not necessary to Mirandize me. Not that it would have mattered. Not with my big mouth.

"Please describe your conversation."

"I asked him to fill in gaps in the timeline we were establishing for the movements of Ms. Baylins and him in the last 24 hours. I told him we knew when they checked into the hotel, when they went to dinner and returned. We knew about the argument that began at the restaurant and continued back at the hotel. The argument seemed odd because, as I mentioned to him, we believed from a vaginal exam of the decedent that the couple had sex after checking into the hotel."

"What was the defendant's reaction to your statement?"

"Mr. Lassiter said, 'This sex we had. Was it good for me?'"

Two of the jurors gasped audibly. Like I said, never let a cop repeat your lousy jokes on the witness stand. They only get worse in the re-telling.

"So Mr. Lassiter made this odd remark while his former lover was lying dead on the floor, strangled?"

"He did."

Judging from their facial expressions, of the twelve jurors, at least eight seemed ready to string me up.

"What happened next?"

"I told Mr. Lassiter that the maître d', the server, and the couple next to them at the restaurant all heard them arguing. As did the taxi driver on the way back to the hotel. I told him that the video camera at the hotel front door picked up the continuation of the argument and that a lip reader could make out Ms. Baylins saying, 'Fuck you, Jake,' as they walked into the hotel."

"What was Mr. Lassiter's reaction?"

"He made another joke."

The jury was transfixed. Just what was this sick comic coming up with now?

"Mr. Lassiter said, 'If I killed every woman who told me the same thing, I'd be in the books with Jack the Ripper.'"

This time, I counted 10 jurors ready to hit the button that would inject me with potassium chloride. And here was the chicken-shit state, only seeking life in prison without parole.

Emilia spent the next several minutes ruling out a forcible rape/murder scenario. There were no signs of a struggle, no bruising, and no defensive wounds. Examination of intact sperm cells and the acid phosphatase test allowed the medical examiner's office to establish the time of sexual intercourse as 24 to 36 hours prior to death, further ruling out an intruder/rapist.

Emilia spent the rest of her examination of Detective Barrios showing how damn brilliant he was, tying together all the pieces of evidence that pointed clearly and exclusively at Jacob Lassiter, attorney at law, killer, and wisecracker. I admitted Pam raked her fingernails across my cheek, leaving the bloody scratch. I admitted being drunk. I denied striking Pamela or harming her in any way. I claimed to have left the suite with Pamela very much alive, though I couldn't place the time.

"Did Mr. Lassiter seem evasive about when he left the hotel for his walk on the beach?"

"Objection, leading," Willow said.

"Sustained."

"Did Mr. Lassiter's vagueness about when he left the hotel mean anything to you, as an experienced homicide detective?"

"Objection, calls for speculation."

"Overruled. You may answer, Detective."

"Mr. Lassiter being a lawyer and all, it just seemed to me he wasn't going to say when he left the hotel until the medical examiner established time of death."

Ouch. Double ouch because it was true.

"Did Mr. Lassiter say why he left the suite?"

"He said he'd been drinking a lot and wanted to clear his head. Indicated it was Pamela's idea."

True. I said it and I'd meant it. Too bad it wasn't a great alibi. Who goes walking on the beach alone in the middle of the night, then falls asleep inches from the shoreline?

Barrios did not break a sweat on Willow's cross exam. Sure, he admitted, Mr. Lassiter said his poor attempts at humor were his way of dealing with grief. *No one on the jury seemed to empathize with my method of mourning.*

"Isn't it true that your entire case against Mr. Lassiter is circumstantial?"

It's a question a lot of defense lawyers ask. Television shows seem to have given circumstantial evidence a bad name. In truth, a strong circumstantial case, backed by forensics, is often stronger than eyewitness testimony, which can so often be shaken in cross examination.

"That's true, Ms. Marsh," Barrios said, confidently. "But in this case, the circumstances are strong, corroborated, and without contradiction. It's as strong a circumstantial case as I've seen in 30 years on the job"

29

The Non-Denial Denial

Life is so damn unfair.

Eddie Novak and Carlos Castillo were crooks and, to a lesser degree, so was Mitch Crowder.

Pam didn't catch me stealing from the trust account; I caught her. Pam was cheating on me, not the other way around, and if I had caught her, I wouldn't have killed her. I would have broken up with her.

But here I was, in the dock for murder.

The horror *du jour* was Barry Samchick, a guy who wanted to help me but was scared to death of Carlos Castillo. When Samchick walked into the courtroom, he avoided making eye contact with me. Always a bad sign. His hearing had improved but his mood hadn't. Affixed with hearing aids, he answered Emilia Vazquez's questions a little louder than necessary.

Yes, he was a C.P.A. who had done my books for the past eleven years. Both my firm's operating accounts and trust accounts were under his purview. He explained that operating accounts were my money and trust accounts were funds being held for clients. Those sums could include settlements of cases not ready to be disbursed, deposits for costs, and the biggie: huge amounts flowing in and out due to the buying and selling of commercial and residential real estate.

No, Samchick could not make transfers from any of the accounts. All checks had to be signed by Jake Lassiter, and all electronic transfers could be made only by someone with the password, that someone again being solely the defendant. Yes, that's the man sitting at the defense table in the dark suit with his shirt a little too small for his neck. Only Jake Lassiter had the password.

"On Saturday June 8 of this year, did you have occasion to speak to the defendant?"

"I called him on his cell phone in the evening."

"A business call?"

"Definitely."

"Even though it was a Saturday night."

"It was important."

"Why was that, Mr. Samchick?"

"I'd been working that day on Jake's accounts and noticed discrepancies in the trust accounts. I called him around nine o'clock. He was at a restaurant with Ms. Baylins."

"What was the defendant's reaction to your revelations?"

"He professed to be shocked."

I didn't like the way he said "professed." As if I were acting.

Whose side are you on, Barry?

"Did you also write the defendant an email that night?"

"Yes. An hour or so later, after I had a chance to review the records in more detail, I sent him an email delineating which accounts had unexplained transfers."

"Was money missing?"

"Technically, there were no shortfalls. Money was transferred out of the trust accounts to banks in the Caymans where it was deposited into literally dozens of Novak Global accounts. The funds were then transferred to other banks. Bermuda. Isle of Man. Singapore. Colombia. Eventually, the original amounts taken from the Lassiter trust accounts flowed back to them, most often from third-party banks."

"Sounds complicated."

"Very difficult to trace."

"What did this lead you to conclude?"

"The accounts being skimmed, the proceeds invested and laundered, the profits retained, and the principal returned."

"And how did you discover this?"

"On one occasion, too much money was returned to a client's account, most likely by accident. When I looked behind the transaction, I found hundreds of others, in and out of the accounts, though in perfect balance."

So far, no lies. I was thankful for that.

"Did you receive a reply from the defendant to your email?"

"Not directly. The next morning, Mr. Lassiter called me from his car, saying he had to see me."

"What can you recall about that phone conversation?"

"Oh, I recall it pretty much verbatim."

And he did. Telling Emilia, the jury, the judge, and the whole damn world exactly what we said to each other as I was barreling down I-95 the morning Pam was killed:

"I don't think you're a thief, Jake."

"Thanks, Barry."

"But murder? That I can see you doing."

"What's that mean?"

"You have a temper."

"The hell I do!"

Samchick was going out of his way to bury me. Whatever happened to the safe, reliable help-your-buddy phrase: *"I don't remember?"* Best I could figure, Samchick was scared shitless of offending one Carlos Castillo, whose name he was loathe to mention. Those trust account funds that had played international traveler – all Castillo's money – not that you would know it from Samchick's testimony.

"When is the next time you saw the defendant?" Emilia Vazquez asked.

"Later that day we met and discussed the accounts."

"Did Mr. Lassiter give you an explanation for the discrepancies?"

"Actually, he asked how this could have happened. I told him only he could have done it because these were all electronic transfers accomplished with a password only he was privy to."

No, dammit, Barry. You never told me that.

As I recall, Samchick had agreed with me that Pamela had somehow gotten my password. But today, my bean counter had the heart of a chicken.

"What was the defendant's reaction to your statement?"

"Anger. He said Pamela must have done it, and that they quarreled violently about it. She accused him of skimming the accounts and he accused her of the same."

"Quarreled *violently*," Emilia repeated. "Did the defendant use that word?"

"He showed me a fresh scratch on his face and said Pamela had basically attacked him in a rage."

Righteous indignation, the jury doubtless thought.

"Did he deny killing her?"

"Well, that's the funny thing."

Oh shit, Barry, now what?

"Funny?" Emilia asked, eyebrows raised.

"I asked him if he killed her and he said, 'You know better than to ask a damn fool question like that.'"

Several jurors shook their heads. In anger? Disbelief? Who knows what?

Samchick wasn't lying. That's exactly what I had said. I had meant it as a denial, sort of saying — *Are you fucking kidding?*" — but out of context, it came off as slippery, as a way of saying *You don't want to know the answer.* A non-denial denial.

"Your witness," Emilia said to Willow with a wicked smile.

I heard Willow sigh before she said to the judge, "May we have one moment, Your Honor?"

"Of course."

Willow leaned in close and whispered. "I'm going to let him go."

"What? The bastard just buried me. He's been threatened by Castillo. He knows in his heart that Pam got the password somehow."

"And you think he'll admit that when I have no way to rebut. I can call him as an adverse witness on our side of the case, after we've had time to put some things together."

"No way!" I was a little too loud, and the jurors strained to hear my privileged, sacrosanct, and pissed-off conversation. "We can't let the jury go home with this as the last thing they hear today."

"Jake, try being a client and not the lawyer, okay? I'm not ready to cross him."

"You should be!"

Willow gave me a withering look and got to her feet. "Your Honor at this time, we have no questions, subject to our right to call Mr. Samchick–"

"Now!" I planted both hands on the defense table and rose to my feet. "We'll cross Mr. Samchick now, and by 'we,' I mean me. I'll be handling the cross, Your Honor."

"No, he won't," Willow fired back.

Judge Marjorie Cohen-Wang gave us a tolerant smile. "If you two want to take five minutes to hash out your situation, please–"

"I'm ready to roll, Your Honor," I interrupted, a no-no in any courtroom.

"I can't allow my client to take an action deleterious to his position," Willow said, calmly.

"In *Faretta versus California,* the United States Supreme Court held that a defendant has a constitutional right to represent himself," I said, proud as hell to have remembered the name of the case.

The judge pursed her lips and nodded, impressed with my off-the-cuff citation of the nearly 40-year-old case in which an alleged thief named Anthony Faretta insisted on defending himself. The Supremes said he could damn well do it. "Mr. Lassiter is correct, Ms. Marsh. So perhaps you should sit down, and let's see what your client has on his mind."

30

The Lure of Filthy Lucre

Facing Barry Samchick on the witness stand, I stood and buttoned my suit coat, noticing it was a little tight around the gut. Granny had been right. I'd gotten pudgy and soft. A guy who back in college used to hoist beer kegs – full, not empty – in each hand. But now…

Money had weakened me.

All those lean years of scrambling for fees in this very building, collecting sweaty wads of cash in the parking lot to handle arraignments and preliminary hearings. Some larger fees as I matured and hauled in bigger cases, but cash flow was always a problem. Then, along came Castillo. Easy money. A staff to process the real estate transactions, a banker and an accountant to oversee the accounts.

I'd gotten lazy.

Ah, the seduction of money. Somewhere in the Bible – don't ask me where – is the admonition, "not given to wine, not greedy of filthy lucre."

Well, I'd violated both tenets. Expensive Champagne and expensive toys. There was my ludicrous Bentley, now under a tarp as much to hide it as to protect its shine. Sure, I could blame Pamela for the car. She's the one who encouraged the purchase and financed it through the bank. The car wasn't me. It was a reflection of a false me.

My thoughts turned to Samchick. That day I found him with his ears boxed. His red Lamborghini had been parked in front of his office bungalow. A ridiculous car for the middle-aged C.P.A., a far cry from the series of hybrids he'd driven for the past decade.

The lure of filthy lucre. I would use my own experience to question him. Just as Novak's bottomless pit of Ponzi money had seduced Pam, Castillo's money had been the kryptonite that had robbed me of my work ethic.

What seduced you, Samchick?

I decided to start conversationally. "How you doing, Barry? You don't mind if I call you Barry?"

"Not a problem. Not so great right now, Jake."

"Ears bothering you?"

"A little, thanks for asking."

"Want to tell the jury how you got hurt?"

"Two guys beat me up and trashed my office."

"Who were those guys?"

"I don't know Jake. Never saw them before."

"They stole the reports you prepared for this case, didn't they?"

That made the jury sit up straight.

"Yes, they did."

"You were going to be a witness for me, weren't you Barry?"

"We'd talked about it, yes."

"But after you were beaten up, you were called by the state?"

"The way it turned out, yeah."

"Those guys who beat you up, did they say anything?"

"Not that I recall."

Certainly a lie, but all I could do was suggest an answer.

"They didn't say, 'This is a message from Carlos Castillo?'"

"I don't remember anything like that."

"Did they ever say, 'You mention Carlos Castillo in court you're a dead man, or words to that effect?'"

"Don't remember anything like that, either, Jake."

I was trying to plant little seeds with the jury that might grow into the tree of reasonable doubt. And poor Barry Samchick was lying his cowardly ass off.

"Let's talk about your Lamborghini."

"What?"

"Your red Lamborghini. The two-passenger Aventador roadster, zero to 60 in 2.9 seconds, if you're so inclined."

"Objection, irrelevant." Emilia didn't know where I was headed and truth be told, neither did I.

"I'll tie it up," I told the judge confidently. That's lawyer talk indicating that somewhere down the road, there's a nexus between seemingly irrelevant questions about a snappy little roadster and the issue of Pam's death.

"Overruled. But make your point quickly, Mr. Lassiter."

"You do own such a car, Barry?"

"The Lamborghini, yes."

"Which you bought after your divorce?"

"Yes. Last year."

"What did that set you back, half a million?"

"Five hundred thirty-five thousand."

The jurors exchanged glances. Just what was going on with this beaten up, spendthrift accountant?

"Did you buy the car for cash?"

"No, I financed it."

"Let me guess. Pamela Baylins handled the financing at Great Southern Bank."

"She did."

"And what are the payments?"

"About $13,000 a month."

Some jurors' eyebrows arched toward the ceiling. I could swear I heard one whistle.

"Where'd that money come from, Barry?"

"Renewed objection!" Emilia said, getting to her feet. "I fail to see what this has to do with whether the defendant committed murder."

So kind of Emilia to remind the jury about all that.

"Mr. Lassiter?" the judge prompted me.

"Your Honor, just a couple more questions will clarify everything."

Beside me, Willow stifled a feminine snort.

"For now, I'm giving you latitude, but please tie it up," the judge said. "Mr. Samchick, you may answer the question."

"The money came from my clients, of course."

"You certainly weren't making that kind of money from me."

"Of course not. But I had other clients."

"Like Eddie Novak, owner of Novak Global Investments."

Samchick just sat there. I could read his mind: *How much does Jake know?*

Not everything. But when I saw the stack of Novak Global prospectuses in Samchick's trashed office, fireworks started to go off. Not one prospectus, as if he'd been studying the figures to invest himself. No, a dozen or so, which could only mean one thing. Samchick was putting his people – his own accounting clients – into Novak's fund.

Into a Ponzi scheme.

But did Samchick know about the fraud?

"Barry, should I repeat the question? Was Eddie Novak a client?"

"Mr. Novak, yes, in a way."

"What does that mean?"

"I don't do the accounting for Novak Global. Let's be clear about that."

Understood. Barry wanted to stay as far away from Global's finances as he could. Meaning at some point, he knew!

"Do you do his personal accounting?"

"No, not that, either."

"But he pays you fees?"

Samchick hesitated, and I filled in the space. "Or commissions, Barry? Does he pay you commissions for placing investors with his fund?"

A bashful "yes" from the witness.

"Let me guess again. You were introduced to Eddie Novak by Pamela Baylins."

"That's right."

"And she suggested you could make commissions by sending Novak investors?"

"Yes."

"What due diligence did you do on your clients' behalf?"

"I relied on the public filings with the S.E.C. like any other investor would do. Plus Pam's personal recommendation. Based on all that, I put my own money into Global and guided some of my clients into the fund as well."

"In return for those commissions you mentioned?"

"Yes, of course."

"How much Barry? Five per cent? Ten per cent of the investments?"

He licked his lips before answering, "One-third. Thirty three and a third per cent."

That stirred the courtroom.

"Helluva commission," I said.

Judge Cohen-Wang waggled a finger at me. "Is that a question, Mr. Lassiter?"

"Sorry, Your Honor."

I decided it was now or never. "Tell the jury, Barry. All this referring of clients you did to Novak Global. Was that before or after you discovered that Global was a scam? A pyramid? A Ponzi scheme?"

The judge sat straighter in her high-backed chair. The jurors stirred, and a murmur went through the gallery. Eddie Novak was a major philanthropist around town, and Novak Global had been the subject of glowing reports in the business section of The Miami Herald. To date, no one had publicly mentioned the possibility that the guy was a junior varsity Bernie Madoff.

"As I said, I relied on Global's public filings."

"C'mon Barry, you relied on that obscene one-third commission. You closed your eyes to the truth until Pam told you it was a Ponzi scheme.

Maybe she even showed you the numbers. Either way, you must have crapped your drawers."

"Mr. Lassiter," the judge cautioned. "Please refrain from scatological references, and please ask questions without making speeches."

"Sorry, Your Honor. Barry, did Pam Baylins tell you Novak was running a Ponzi scheme?"

"Objection. Hearsay." Emilia didn't seem to have her heart in it.

"Overruled," the judge said, wanting to hear the answer.

"Pam did." Barry sighed, took a breath, seemed to think it over, and then the floodgates opened. "Just a few days before she was killed. She'd somehow gotten the real financials. Novak wasn't trading currencies and wasn't making investments. None at all. He was just paying off earlier investors with later investors' money. The books said Novak controlled about a billion in assets when there was barely 75 million that could be gathered when the end would come, as it surely would. And those monies would pretty much go to the lawyers and accountants."

"Leaving you and Pam with similar problems, isn't that right Barry? She had Carlos Castillo's money invested with Novak and you had what, a couple dozen clients along for the ride?"

"Thirty-seven clients, plus $700,000 of my own money, which on the books was supposedly worth $3 million or so, but in reality, in the event of a run on the fund, was worth *bupkes,* nothing."

"So why'd you call me that Saturday night about my trust accounts? They seemed to be the least of your problems."

"I was putting out fires. The Florida Bar had an audit scheduled of your accounts. They would have discovered the discrepancies, and that would have led to Novak Global. I thought we could buy time with just a couple transfers to even the inflow and outflow on your accounts. I wasn't ready for the axe to fall on Novak Global."

"Five days earlier, which was the day after she learned that Novak Global was a Ponzi scheme, Pam got Castillo's money out. But you didn't take out yours or your clients' investments. Why is that?"

Samchick slumped in the witness chair. "In this day and age, the news would have spread instantly. There'd have been a run. Global would have gone under in a day. Even if my clients got out some of their money, the trustee in bankruptcy would have filed clawback suits to get it back. I'd have been sued, maybe criminally prosecuted, even though I knew nothing of the fraud until it was too late."

"So you and Pam tried to agree on a strategy?"

"I wanted to buy time. She wanted to make a whistle blower's complaint to the S.E.C. She figured if the trustee could round up what was still in the accounts…"

"Seventy-five million."

"Right. She'd get a reward in the five to seven million dollar range."

"Whereas you wanted to wait, but for what, Barry?"

"I talked to Eddie Novak. Told him what I knew. He pleaded for time. He said he could always solicit new investors. They were falling all over each other to get in. He thought he could keep the fund going for 25 or 30 years, just like Madoff did. He told me that paying off Pam to keep her quiet would be no problem. He could go higher than any whistle blower fee."

"But there was a problem, wasn't there?"

"She was afraid of being charged with conspiracy. She wouldn't go along."

"Is that why you killed her, Barry?"

A collective gasp came from the jurors.

"I didn't kill her."

"C'mon, Barry. You just confessed to motive."

"Jesus, Jake. You, more than anyone else, know that I'm not capable of that. I didn't kill Pam. Eddie Novak did."

31

Lobby Rats

"Objection! No foundation. Rank speculation. Invades the province of the jury. Move to strike the witness's answer." Emilia Vazquez was one unhappy prosecutor.

"Sustained on the ground of foundation," Judge Cohen-Wang ruled quickly. "The jury shall disregard the last answer after the words, 'I didn't kill Pam.'"

Judge's instructions to disregard are hard as hell for jurors to follow. Try, for example, at this very moment, *not* thinking of an elephant. Still, to get Samchick's accusation into evidence, there were certain rules to follow, certain foundations to be laid. I would do my best.

"Barry, did you see Eddie Novak kill Pamela?"
"No."
"Were you present when she was killed?"
"No."
"Did Eddie Novak tell you he killed her?"
"No."

Well, this isn't going so hot.

"On what basis do you conclude that Eddie Novak killed Pam?"

"Objection to the form of the question. Assumes a fact not in evidence and calls for speculation." Emilia was not going to take my cross exam sitting down.

"Sustained. Try again, Mr. Lassiter."

That's the thing about the so-called justice system. It's not really a search for the truth as that cheesy sign above the judge's bench says. It's a narrow inquiry into whether the state can prove that a particular defendant committed a crime. Getting proof into evidence that someone else did the crime is a high wire act.

Let me admit something right now. I wasn't doing a very good job. As the old saying goes about people who represent themselves, I had a fool for a client. I was also rusty. My newfound status as a real estate lawyer had kept me out of criminal court. But I had come this far and I wasn't giving up. I needed to *properly* get into evidence Samchick's statement that Eddie Novak killed Pam. Problem was…Samchick seemed to be simply assuming Novak did.

When a lawyer absolutely doesn't know what to ask, the confused mouthpiece can always resort to a form of "What happened next?" And so I did.

"Barry, after you called me at the restaurant around 9 p.m. on Saturday night June 8, what did you do?"

"Like I told the prosecutor, I probed into more detail on your accounts and then emailed you."

"Then what did you do?"

He paused a long moment. "I called Eddie Novak and told him about the problem. All the problems. The Florida Bar could uncover the whole deal with its audit. Pam could blow the whistle for the reward. You could find out and start punching people. A certain dangerous Latin American investor could find out, and Novak and me could disappear without a trace."

"Did you come up with a solution to all these problems?"

"Novak said–"

"Objection, hearsay!" Emilia stayed on her feet, ready for her next objection.

"Sustained."

"Barry, without telling us what Mr. Novak said, did you come up with a plan?"

"Yes, sort of. But it didn't involve killing anybody."

"Okay, what was the plan?"

"Like I said, bribery. We were gonna pay Pam to keep her mouth shut."

"How were you going to do that?"

"By moving quickly. Novak and I met in the lobby of the Fontainebleau around midnight. I called your suite from a house phone in the lobby. You answered. In the background, I could hear Pam screaming at you. I decided this might not be the best time for our meeting, so I hung up."

"Then what happened?"

"We had a drink in one of the hotel bars. Around 2 a.m., we saw you get out of an elevator and stagger toward the doors to the beach. You never saw us. The way you looked, you barely knew where you were. As we're trying to figure out what to do, in walked Mitch Crowder. Novak recognized him right away, and for the life of us, we couldn't figure what's going on. Crowder took the elevator, presumably to your suite. He's not up there long. Maybe between 2:30 and 2:45, he leaves, and Novak says–"

"Objection, hearsay."

"Sustained."

"Without telling us what Novak says, what does he do?"

"We know you're not in the suite, Jake, so we figure this is our chance. I stay in the lobby. Novak goes to the suite to talk to her. To offer her ten million dollars. At the time, he didn't know she'd already written the email to her bosses at the bank and set the wheels in motion to notify the S.E.C. about the Ponzi scheme. Novak must have lost it because when he comes down, he says, 'She won't be spilling no beans.'"

"Objection, hearsay. Move to strike." Emilia was still on her feet.

"Sustained. The jury shall disregard the witness's last sentence."

"Sorry, Judge," Samchick said.

"When Novak came down from the suite," I said, "without saying what he said, what was your impression of how things stood?"

"Well, Novak left me with the impression that our problems were over."

"Because he'd paid off Pamela?"

"No. Because she wouldn't be around anymore to blow the whistle."

"Because she was dead?"

"That was my impression."

"And I'd be blamed for her murder?"

"Jesus, Jake, I'm sorry."

"Nothing further," I said, like the old pro I was.

Judge Cohen-Wang seemed to sigh before addressing Emilia Vazquez. "I assume the state wishes to question the witness on re-direct."

Which was sort of like saying, I assume Pope Francis is Catholic.

"Your Honor, we wish first to declare Mr. Samchick an adverse witness so we can cross-examine. Second, we ask the Court to admonish the witness on the penalties for perjury."

"Objection!" Both Willow and I were on our feet simultaneously.

The judge smiled tolerantly in our direction. "One of you sit down. I'll leave it to the two of you to decide which one."

Being the gentlemanly type, I took my seat, and Willow said, "The prosecutor's self-serving statement was intended both to intimidate the witness and prejudice the jury. It is *she* who should be admonished."

The judge sighed, checked the clock on the wall, which read half-past-five, and said, "It's been a long, trying day. No pun intended. We'll recess now. Everyone get a good night's sleep, and the state can begin its re-direct tomorrow. The jury is excused with the same admonitions as always. Counsel, when the jury has left, please approach the bench."

We all stood. The jury filed out. Emilia, Willow, and I sauntered up to the bench. "I asked for counsel," the judge said. "Why are you here, Mr. Lassiter?"

"Oh, I just presumed…"

"I run a courtroom, not a circus. Now I have no idea if you and the witness cooked up that little story or if you were just winging it…"

"Flying by the seat of my pants, Your Honor."

"Either way, when we resume tomorrow, you keep those pants stuck to your chair, you understand?"

"Yes, Your Honor."

"Now, anything else? Ms. Vazquez?"

"We renew our objection to the witness's statement that Mr. Novak committed the murder. As Mr. Lassiter's own questions revealed, the witness saw nothing and Mr. Novak admitted nothing. The witness was left with 'impressions.' Needless to say, 'impressions' are not evidence, certainly not evidence of the commission of murder. It therefore follows that all of the witness's testimony about what may have happened in the suite should be stricken. The witness wasn't there. His testimony was entirely speculation and hocus-pocus."

It only took the judge a moment. "Objection sustained. I will instruct the jury tomorrow to disregard the testimony. Currently, there is no evidence before the jury that Mr. Novak, a third party to these proceedings, admitted the killing, either directly or by inference."

I stifled my un-lawyerly urge to shout, *"Are you fucking kidding me? I just elicited reasonable doubt, evidence that Some Other Dude Did It."*

"Have a good night, everyone," the judge told us, before standing and fleeing the bench, her black robes sailing behind her.

32

La Verdad

On the way out of the courthouse, I ran into Detective George Barrios. "Nice job, shyster," he said to me.

"If that's a compliment, thanks."

"I mean it. If I'm ever rightfully accused, I'll hire you."

"You mean wrongfully accused."

"If I'm innocent, why would I need a slick-as-owl-shit shyster like you?"

"You know Novak is gonna skedaddle, don't you?"

"Not my problem."

"He killed my girlfriend."

"Your cheating, thieving girlfriend, you mean."

"A living, breathing human being."

"Why don't you go make a citizen's arrest?"

"I wouldn't arrest him. I'd beat him to a pulp."

"Good. We'll add that to the charges against you."

"Something else you gotta do, give Barry Samchick protection."

"What do I look like, a bouncer at a South Beach club?"

"Carlos Castillo is gonna be unhappy with him. Does that register with you?"

"I'm a homicide detective, Lassiter. Call me if you've got a body, preferably one within the city limits of Miami Beach."

"Don't be a dick, Barrios."

"Look, your pal Samchick wanted to be in business with Novak and Castillo. Now, he's gotta deal with it."

❦

The murder trial had barely caused a ripple in the news. Sure, there was some local interest in a lawyer accused of killing his lover. *The Miami Herald* and the local television stations gave sporadic coverage. But now, the national news media and the Internet were blazing. A witness under oath had claimed that Novak Global was a Ponzi scheme and Novak himself might be a murderer. The news media were not burdened by the same rules of evidence that guided Judge Cohen-Wang. My cell phone was ringing with reporters from around the country. CNN had the story within an hour. On HLN, Nancy Grace had broken out in hives.

Within an hour, Novak Global released a statement denying all claims and saying it would produce its audited financial statements within two days. Just enough time, I figured, for Novak to skip to some lovely country with no extradition treaty. It's not as if the cops were on their way to arrest him, based on the stricken-as-hearsay testimony of Barry Samchick.

The state is loathe to ever admit its mistakes. Just ask the plethora of inmates who were later exonerated, despite vigorous attempts by the state to keep them behind bars. As far as the police and prosecutors were concerned, they had their man, and that was me.

After watching the news and fending off phone calls for a couple hours, I got in the old Caddy, fired up the engine, and headed from my house in the South Grove to Barry Samchick's house in the North Grove. He'd apologized to me in court for helping frame me. With some prodding, he even tried to help me, by pointing the finger at Novak, even if the judge wasn't having any of it. He'd avoided mentioning Castillo by name, but he did make reference to "a certain dangerous Latin American investor."

Maybe I was wrong. Maybe Castillo wouldn't care that Samchick made some oblique reference to him and his dirty money. Maybe the Colombian tough guy had too many other problems. But he had to know that the feds would follow up. Maybe they'd take their own sweet federal time doing it, but I could predict a grand jury subpoena in Barry Samchick's future and an investigation called *"In re Carlos Castillo."*

On the way to his house, I formulated my plan. I would tell Samchick to pack everything he could into his Lamborghini and head north on the Florida Turnpike.

Take lots of cash so no one can trace your credit card charges, and let things simmer down a while before deciding what to do.

Naturally, I didn't tell Willow Marsh what I was about to do. She was still thinking we would re-call Samchick on the defense half of the case. But I was feeling guilty about placing Barry in the bulls-eye, of making my problem his. As for the case, we would have to do without him from here on out.

☙

I parked my old Caddy in front of Samchick's house, and…oh shit. A black Escalade sat next to the Lamborghini. I hurried around to the office bungalow in back. Sure enough, Carlos Castillo was there with two of his bulky thugs in black suits. But this time they weren't boxing Barry Samchick's ears. With the thugs off to one side, Samchick and Castillo were sitting on the front steps of the cottage. Castillo had an arm around Samchick's shoulders.

"Am I interrupting anything?" I asked.

"Jake, Jake, Jake," Castillo said, almost sadly. "What are you doing here?"

"I was just about to ask you the same thing, Carlos."

"Go home, Jake," Barry Samchick said.

"Listen to the man," Castillo said. "He did you a *un gran* favor in court today."

"He told the truth."

"Ah, *la verdad.* I almost forgot. You are the man who keeps searching for the truth but seldom finds it."

"Barry, why are you even talking to this son-of-a-bitch who had you beaten up?"

Samchick just shook his head.

Castillo said, "Because he is smarter than you, this speaker of the truth. He helped you without once mentioning my name, which is more than I can say for you." Castillo shook his head sadly, as if I had disappointed him.

"Be happy, Jake," Samchick said. "You're gonna get off."

"Maybe I will and maybe I won't. The judge isn't helping."

"I will be truly regretful if you are convicted," Castillo said. "What you did for my son was an honorable act, though one which I have repaid many times with my business. And Pamela always spoke so highly of you."

"When? In bed with you?"

"Ah, jealousy. At this late date, let it go."

"I don't know who's a bigger scumbag, Castillo. You or Eddie Novak."

Castillo barked out a small laugh. "Oh, I assure you that Novak is what you would call a bush leaguer compared to me. Do you know the things I have done to get as rich as I am?"

"I can only guess."

"Novak's solution to our problem was to pay bribes. Pay Pamela? What would that solve? She would still know about Novak's Ponzi scheme and my laundered money. What would we do when she wanted more money? Or what would keep her from taking our money and still going to the FBI and S.E.C. for whistle blower rewards, maybe get herself into Witness Protection? The dangers were far too great."

"So you knew Novak was going to kill her, you bastard?"

Castillo's eyes turned as hard and cold as a glacier. "Tell him, Samchick. Tell this clever lawyer what he wants, *la verdad.*"

Samchick shook his head.

"Tell him!"

"Eddie Novak didn't kill Pam."

"What!" I said.

"Eddie Novak a killer?" Castillo laughed at the notion. "With his bare hands and a belt? It's ridiculous."

"He's strong enough," I said.

"The man has gym muscles, not street muscles. He's not a bone breaker, he does Pilates! He juggles numbers for a living."

"On the stand today, Barry, who were you protecting?" Thinking immediately it was a stupid question, that the answer was right there in front of me.

Novak wasn't a Natural Born Killer. But Castillo…

"I was already in the suite when Novak came in," Castillo said, suppressing a fuck-you smile. "He watched while I picked up your belt, and when I grabbed Pam by the hair, Novak turned and ran for the elevators like a little girl. He never even heard her scream."

"You bastard!" The anger smoldered inside of me.

"Do you know I fucked her the day before you took her to the hotel? How's that make you feel, *idiota?*"

"Like you're a scumbag." The anger had turned to fury, and it dug into my skull like a drill bit.

"You know what Pamela's last words were? 'Jake! Help me, Jake!'"

That was it. I lunged for him, just as he knew I would. From nowhere, he produced a blade and swiped at my mid-section, grazing me but barely drawing blood. His two thugs approached but Castillo waved them off with the knife. He came at me again with a thrust. I caught his right wrist with my left hand, swung my right hand to his elbow and yanked his arm down hard while I came up with a knee. His right forearm *snapped* across my knee and he yelled something unintelligible as the knife dropped to the ground.

I got off two punches, a short right upper-cut flush to his jaw, then a downward strike to the back of his head with both my hands locked. He dropped straight as a stone to the ground.

It took about one more second for the two thugs to grab me and begin pummeling my face with a flurry of fists. Two seconds later, a gunshot stopped everyone.

I had dropped to a knee and looked up to see Detective George Barrios with a nine millimeter handgun pointed at the thugs.

"Either of you two move, you're dead. Jake, we got everything on tape. Samchick's wired. The bushes are wired. If it had been up to me, your ankle bracelet would have been wired."

Barrios turned to Castillo, who was moaning, cradling his broken right arm in his left, and looking stunned. "Carlos Castillo, you're under arrest for the murder of Pamela Baylins. You have the right to an attorney. If you cannot afford an attorney, one will be provided for you. You have the right to remain silent. Anything you say or do can and will be used against you in a court of law."

Barrios looked toward me. "Ain't that right, Jake?"

Epilogue

Barefoot and wearing an orange jumpsuit with "City of Miami Beach" lettered across the back, I was wielding a heavy metal rake. I had a four-day growth of stubble and smelled of salt and sweat. My face was still bruised from the mini-beating. My amiable caveman look.

It was just after sunrise and Miami Beach was already steamy along the shoreline at Tenth Street.

My high-priced lawyer, the classy Ms. Marsh, had a difficult time getting the murder charges dismissed, if you can believe that. Emilia Vazquez played hard ass, even though she had a taped confession from Carlos Castillo. Here's a statistic to chew on. About 25 percent of death row in-mates who are later exonerated have confessed to the crime they did not commit. That's usually a statistic bandied about by defense lawyers. But in this case, that's what the prosecutor told the judge about Castillo's statement. Emilia demanded I plead guilty to *something* in exchange for the deal.

The real reason was so that the state didn't look so damn stupid.

I copped a plea to camping overnight on the beach, a municipal offense that didn't even rise to the level of a misdemeanor. My sentence was 30 hours raking seaweed, dead birds, and used condoms into piles where half-tracks could pick up the detritus and haul it away.

On this day, with the sun sizzling just above the horizon, only a few joggers splashed along the shorebreak. Your usual collection of leggy SoBe models in bikinis, some male bodybuilders, and a few oldsters with skin baked the color of cordovan loafers. On the beach, two male retirees swept at the sand with metal detectors, looking for lost Rolexes, but uncovering mostly bird shit.

Coming toward me was a tattooed muscular young man in red Speedos. When he got closer, I recognized Mitch Crowder. He slowed, kept jogging in place, and said, "At last, Lassiter, you've found your calling."

"How you doing, pal?"

"Great. I put in a claim as a whistle blower on Novak Global."

"You?"

"I'm the guy who got the real documents and uncovered the fraud, remember?"

"By illegal hacking."

"Government doesn't care once I turned over everything I had. Reward's gonna be maybe 5 mil."

With that, he resumed jogging, kicking up sand. My financial circumstances were different. With the fortune Willow charged me and no new cases from the day I was charged with murder, I'd have to rebuild my practice from square one.

I'd gotten the bad news about my finances from Barry Samchick. Yeah, I still retained him as my accountant. He found a guy to buy my dumb-ass Bentley and his Lamborghini in one transaction. We both lost money, but what was new about that? Without charging him a fee, I worked out a deal for Samchick to get immunity to testify against Novak in the Ponzi scheme case.

Novak had been arrested at Tamiami Airport, trying to board his private jet for Buenos Aries. He was facing 50 years for his scam.

Castillo was being held without bail for the first degree murder of Pamela plus about 300 counts of money laundering. That son-of-a-bitch would never see a sunrise again.

I kept raking until the heat and humidity got to me. Against regulations, I stripped off my jump-suit. I wore a pair of old green University of Miami swim trunks underneath. Near 11th Street, I nearly stumbled across a woman lying in the sand. She wore yellow bikini bottoms and a man's long sleeve white shirt. Mid-thirties, tanned, dark hair, and long, strong runner's legs.

Sleeping.

Whether she had spent the night in violation of the City Code or had come to the beach early, I couldn't tell.

"Excuse me," I said. "You gotta get up."

She opened bleary eyes, covered her face with a hand and stared up at me. It was not the look Brad Pitt would have gotten had he awakened her.

"You can't sleep here," I said. "A half-track is coming by to pick up the seaweed crap."

"Fuck off."

"Really. It's dangerous. And if you were here all night, that's a municipal offense."

She propped herself up on an elbow and studied me. "What kind of jerkoff are you?"

"The usual kind."

"No, really. You don't push a rake for a living, do you?"

"How would you know?"

She let me have a sleepy little smile. "Because you have a sixty-dollar haircut and you don't have calluses on your hands. But your nose was broken once."

"Twice."

"Rough around the edges, but all in all, an interesting look."

"And you are…?"

"Holly Knight. Like Holy Night, but with an extra 'l.'"

"You pay attention to details, don't you Holly with an extra l?"

"I have to. I'm a private investigator. And you?"

"Jake Lassiter. Parolee."

"Oh, Lassiter. The guy who didn't kill his girl-friend."

"Not yet."

"You want to go for a swim, Jake?"

"Sure."

"I'll race you to Fifth Street and back. Loser buys breakfast."

"Deal."

She stripped out of the white shirt. No bikini top. Just a fine pair of small, round breasts not quite as tanned as the rest of her. I wasn't sure, but I figured she might be violating another Miami Beach ordinance.

We jogged into the churning surf, diving into the shorebreak. She swam with long strokes and a strong kick. I would be buying breakfast.

I squinted as I swam, the sun glinting off the turquoise water. With each moment, the sun rose higher over the Atlantic. I lifted my head and saw that Holly had slowed down to let me pull along-side. She flipped over and did long, languorous backstrokes, her body sleek and glowing in the morning light.

I kept chugging along in my version of the crawl. With each stroke, I felt cleansed, the past washing off me, the morning sun lighting a path of new possibilities. I was looking forward to pancakes and bacon with the lady. Then, I would haul ass to the office and get back to work. Somewhere in the city, there had to be a client or two in need of justice…or a reasonable facsimile thereof.

Best would be a cause that is just, a client I like, and a check that doesn't bounce. On this glorious morning ripe with possibilities and new beginnings, I would settle for two out of three.

THE END

ABOUT THE AUTHOR

The author of 18 novels, Paul Levine won the John D. MacDonald fiction award and was nominated for the Edgar, Macavity, International Thriller, and James Thurber prizes. A former trial lawyer, he also wrote more than 20 episodes of the CBS military drama "JAG" and co-created the Supreme Court drama "First Monday" starring James Garner and Joe Mantegna. The critically acclaimed international bestseller "To Speak for the Dead" was his first novel. He is also the author of the "Solomon vs. Lord" series and the thrillers "Illegal," "Ballistic," "Impact," and "Paydirt." A graduate of Penn State University and the University of Miami Law School, he lives in Miami. You can sign up for the author's free newsletter and be eligible for signed books and more at http://www. paul-levine.com

ALSO AVAILABLE

JAKE LASSITER SERIES

"Mystery writing at its very, very best." – Larry King, USA TODAY

TO SPEAK FOR THE DEAD: Linebacker-turned-lawyer Jake Lassiter begins to believe that his surgeon client is innocent of malpractice…but guilty of murder.

NIGHT VISION: After several women are killed by an Internet stalker, Jake is appointed a special prosecutor, and follows a trail of evidence from Miami to London and the very streets where Jack the Ripper once roamed.

FALSE DAWN: After his client confesses to a murder he didn't commit, Jake follows a bloody trail from Miami to Havana to discover the truth.

MORTAL SIN: Talk about conflicts of interest. Jake is sleeping with Gina Florio and defending her mob-connected husband in court.

RIPTIDE: Jake Lassiter chases a beautiful woman and stolen bonds from Miami to Maui.

FOOL ME TWICE: To clear his name in a murder investigation, Jake follows a trail of evidence that leads from Miami to buried treasure in the abandoned silver mines of Aspen, Colorado. (Also available in a new paperback edition).

FLESH & BONES: Jake falls for his beautiful client even though he doubts her story. She claims to have recovered "repressed memories" of abuse… just before gunning down her father

LASSITER: Jake retraces the steps of a model who went missing 18 years earlier…after his one-night stand with her. (Also available in a new paperback edition).

LAST CHANCE LASSITER: In this prequel novella, young Jake Lassiter has an impossible case: he represents Cadillac Johnson, an aging rhythm and blues musician who claims his greatest song was stolen by a top-of-the-charts hip-hop artist.

SOLOMON vs. LORD SERIES

(Nominated for the Edgar, Macavity, International Thriller, and James Thurber awards).

"A cross between 'Moonlighting' and 'Night Court.' Courtroom drama has never been this much fun." – *FreshFiction.com*

SOLOMON vs. LORD: Trial lawyer Victoria Lord, who follows every rule, and Steve Solomon, who makes up his own, bicker and banter as they defend a beautiful young woman, accused of killing her wealthy, older husband.

THE DEEP BLUE ALIBI: Solomon and Lord come together – and fly apart – defending Victoria's "Uncle Grif" on charges he killed a man with a speargun. It's a case set in the Florida Keys with side trips to coral reefs and a nudist colony where all is more –and less – than it seems.

KILL ALL THE LAWYERS: Just what did Steve Solomon do to infuriate ex-client and ex-con "Dr. Bill?" Did Solomon try to lose the case in which the TV shrink was charged in the death of a woman patient?

HABEAS PORPOISE: It starts with the kidnapping of a pair of trained dolphins and turns into a murder trial with Solomon and Lord on *opposite* sides after Victoria is appointed a special prosecutor, and fireworks follow!

STAND-ALONE THRILLERS

IMPACT: A Jetliner crashes in the Everglades. Is it negligence or terrorism? When the legal case gets to the Supreme Court, the defense has a unique strategy: Kill anyone, even a Supreme Court Justice, to win the case.

BALLISTIC: A nuclear missile, a band of terrorists, and only two people who can prevent Armageddon. A "loose nukes" thriller for the 21st Century. (Also available in a new paperback edition).

ILLEGAL: Down-and-out lawyer Jimmy (Royal) Payne tries to re-unite a Mexican boy with his missing mother and becomes enmeshed in the world of human trafficking and sex slavery.

PAYDIRT: Bobby Gallagher had it all and lost it. Now, assisted by his 12-year-old brainiac son, he tries to rig the Super Bowl, win a huge bet...and avoid getting killed. (Also available in a new paperback edition).

Visit the author's website at http://www.paul-levine.com for more information. While there, sign up for Paul Levine's newsletter and the chance to win free books and other prizes.

9/105

9/15

DISCARD

BRADFORD PUBLIC LIBRARY
P.O. BOX 619
BRADFORD, VT 05033
802 222-4536

23404133R00142

Made in the USA
Middletown, DE
24 August 2015